TIMELESS DEVOTION

KAY P. DAWSON

INTRODUCTION

Timeless Devotion is the tenth book in the Timeless Hearts -Sweet Western Time Travel Series.

This multi-author series ties into one central concept of two women, in different times, who help people find their true love...even if it isn't in their own time.

You can find them all of the books in the series listed on the Amazon author page - amazon.com/author/timelesshearts (Be sure to click "Follow" to be notified of any new releases).

We hope you enjoy the series that will show you love knows no boundaries...even time itself.

Sandra E. Sinclair, Peggy L. Henderson, Anna Rose Leigh & Kay P. Dawson - Timeless Hearts Authors

**Follow us on FB!

CHAPTER 1

"You know, when things don't work out how you'd planned, often it means there is something better out there waiting for you."

Clara listened to the woman speaking to her across the table, while letting her eyes take in the dusty street outside the window. They sat at the small table inside the dining room of Cissie's boardinghouse, where she'd spent the night after arriving in Heartsbridge yesterday.

A couple entered the mercantile across the street, with the man holding the door open for the woman to go through. The way he smiled at her as she passed him made Clara's heart ache with the love she could see reflected in his face. It was the same way she'd seen Gabe Noland look at his new wife yesterday when she'd been introduced to them.

Clara had hoped perhaps coming out here to Texas would give her the chance to have the same thing for herself. She knew it was a foolish, romantic notion. But she'd let herself believe the man she'd been corresponding with for weeks, and who she'd come all this way to marry, would learn to love her too.

However, when she'd arrived, it had been revealed that the man she'd thought she was marrying, was facing trial for numerous crimes. Now she was all alone in Texas, far from her home in Boston—with no family, no money, and nowhere else to go.

She swallowed hard against the lump that was threatening in her throat. *She'd been through worse than this. She would figure something out.*

She repeated the words she'd said over and over in her mind for years, ever since her parents died.

"Truthfully, it's the best thing that could have happened. If you'd arrived on time, and married Martin Paine, I shudder to think how things would have turned out for you." Cissie reached out and took her hand, so Clara turned her eyes

2

away from the window and smiled at the beautiful redhead trying to comfort her.

"I know. I'm grateful I was delayed in coming here. I just wish I knew where I was going to now."

Martin had sent her money for a ticket, and she'd let him know she'd be arriving within a few weeks. But when it came time to leave, her employer, Mrs. Lacy Dunning, had required her to accompany them for a short visit to family, so she hadn't been able to get away as early as she'd hoped.

Clara had been afraid of letting Mr. Dunning find out what she'd planned on doing, so she'd had to oblige. By the time she'd arrived in Hearts-bridge a couple weeks after originally planned, her future husband had already been arrested, and she was left on her own.

Cissie was patting her hand, smiling warmly at her. She was so thankful she'd run into the woman from the boardinghouse as she stepped off the stagecoach. Cissie had let her spend the night, even though Clara didn't have any money. She planned to help with some cooking and cleaning to help pay off her debt.

She let her eyes move back to the street

outside the window as she thought about what she could do. Going back to Boston wasn't an option.

As she watched, the couple she'd met yesterday at their wedding just after she'd arrived in town, and another couple, came walking up the street. One of the women was laughing as she carried an infant on her hip.

Cissie stood up and smiled at them as they opened the door and came inside the boarding-house. "I wondered when you all would be back. Did you get everything cleared up at the courthouse?"

Clara's cheeks warmed as she realized the eyes of the new arrivals were now on her. She knew they were talking about tying up loose ends concerning the man she was supposed to be marrying.

"Everything is finished. Martin has been taken to face the judge in Austin. So, today I'm taking my new wife, and we're headed home. Thanks for letting us stay last night, Cissie." The man she'd met yesterday had his arm around the woman with dark hair, and smiled down at her as he talked.

"Yes, thank you for letting us stay too." The other woman holding the baby spoke. "It would have been too much dragging Henry all the way home, then back again this morning to give our statements, and to see Gabe and Charlotte off." She walked over and put her hand out to Clara.

"My name is Elizabeth Langley. You must be Clara Swanson." Clara shook her hand and nodded.

"I am. I suppose everyone in town knows who I am, I'm afraid." She gave a little laugh to try and ease some of the tension. She knew people were uncomfortable with knowing what to say to her, considering the circumstances she was now facing.

"Would you mind if we join you? We should all have something to eat before we leave for home. And Cissie makes the best pancakes and bacon you'll ever eat." Clara could see the kindness in the other woman's eyes, and welcomed the company of others to help keep her mind off her troubles.

"This is my husband, Noah. And I believe you met Charlotte and Gabe yesterday at their wedding."

After everyone was seated, Cissie came back to the table with mugs for everyone, and a metal coffeepot in her hand.

"We're all terribly sorry for what you're facing

now that Martin has been sent away, but I assure you, we'll all help with whatever you need to get back home." Noah smiled at her with kindness in his eyes. Clara had to choke back the sob that threatened to give her away.

She hadn't known a great deal of kindness in her life, at least not from men. The one person who'd shown her any decency was the woman she'd worked for before coming to Texas. Even though she was her employer, she'd tried to be somewhat of a mother figure to Clara. If not for the rest of Mrs. Dunning's family, Clara knew she'd have been happy to spend the rest of her life working for her.

"I won't be going back to Boston. I will have to figure out how I can make my own way." Her gaze moved to Cissie who was coming back in carrying the plates of pancakes and bacon on a tray. "I was hoping maybe someone might have somewhere I could work until I figure out what to do and where I can go." She knew she wasn't going to be able to hide the desperation from her eyes as she waited to see if Cissie would let her stay there to work.

Cissie smiled at her as she set the tray down, then took the seat next to her, taking one of her hands in her own. "I promised I'd help you. And I know exactly what I can do." She took one hand away to pull out a timepiece on a blue ribbon around her neck from the collar of her dress.

Clara squinted her eyes to get a good look at the beautiful piece she held. The intricate design around the face was stunning, and as she watched, Clara noticed the hands were moving unusually slow. The others around the table let out a gasp, and she became mesmerized by the hands when they started to pick up speed, eventually settling into a smooth rhythm.

She pulled her eyes away and looked up at Cissie.

"What if I told you I could help you get away from here, and to someplace where you can find true happiness? The place you belong," said Cissie.

Clara couldn't understand what she meant, but Clara knew that somehow, her life was about to change.

CHAPTER 2

"Come on, Moira. Just one date. You can't keep finding excuses not to say yes."

Grady Langley rolled his eyes as he lifted another spoonful of the hot soup to his mouth. Duncan Rogers and Harvey Lawrence, two of the men he was working with on this job had been harassing the poor waitresses at the diner they ate at every day. Now, only the owner herself, Moira Lockhart, would serve them.

So now they'd moved onto bothering her.

But Grady smiled as he listened to Moira putting them in their place. "Listen, guys, I've put up with you coming in here and acting like Neanderthals around the other ladies working here. But if you can't learn to behave appropriately, I'm going to have to ask you not to come back. I don't care if you're working on the building across the street. I don't put up with disrespectful heathens treating any of my staff like this. So, either you learn some manners or find somewhere else to eat your lunch."

She turned to walk back into the kitchen, while the men beside him snorted.

As he continued eating, he savored the creaminess of the soup as it slid down his throat. He looked forward to these meals at Moira's Diner every day. She was one of the best cooks around—next to his grandmother—and he wasn't going to let them ruin his chances to eat here while they did this job.

He kept reminding himself this job was only temporary. He had plans, and working in construction would pay the bills while he worked on the dream he had for his grandfather's ranch.

Over the years, they'd worked hard to try and keep the money coming in at the ranch, but things just weren't as prosperous as they'd once been. Grady had always thought after his mom was killed in a car accident, his grandpa had just given up on life and let the ranch fall into a state of disrepair. She'd been the youngest daughter and both of his grandparents mourned their child deeply.

He'd never known his father, only being told he'd left before Grady was born. So, it had been up to his grandparents to take over raising him.

Now that Grady was older, he had plans for the ranch, and wanted to build it up to something that would provide for them both as they got older. It was his turn to look after them now.

"She's pretty uppity. She just needs herself a good man to show her how to behave."

Harvey laughed at his friend's comment. "And I suppose you think that man is you? She won't give you the time of day. You need to be more subtle. Let a real man show you how it's done."

Grady sighed loudly and finally turned his head to look at the other men. He really wasn't in the mood to deal with them, and every day it was the same thing. He'd tell them to back off, and they'd laugh and tune out everything he said. They really were the kind of men who had no respect for women, and thought the sun rose and set with themselves because they normally had girls groveling at their feet.

That is, if the stories they were always telling

everyone else were true, which Grady suspected were highly exaggerated.

"How many more times do you guys need to be rejected by a woman before you realize she's truly not interested? Why not just leave the women in here alone and save all your charming pickup lines for tonight?" Grady knew they went out clubbing just about every night because they always spent the next day talking about their conquests.

Moira came back over, offering a smile to Grady as she poured him another cup of coffee. At least she didn't think he was anything like these guys.

"How are the ranch plans coming along?"

He'd been coming in here for over a month, and he'd gotten to know her enough to talk about some of the plans he had. She was genuinely a caring woman, he could tell that about her right away. And he found himself talking a lot about how he hoped to make it into a successful bed-and-breakfast like the one his cousin managed in Montana.

"It's starting to come together. I'm hoping we can be ready to open things up soon. It's hard doing a lot of it by myself, especially when I only have the weekends and evenings after work to do it."

His grandparents still lived on the ranch in the new house that was built just before he'd gone to live with them as a child. But the old original house on the property was still there, and was a monument to his ancestors who'd passed the farm down to the subsequent generations.

It hadn't been much when it was first built by his great-great grandfather, Noah, after a tornado had destroyed the original cabin they were living in. But he'd heard how over the years as the family had grown, Noah had added on.

Each generation after that had added their own touches, and looked after it, until it was now the big, beautiful old home that had stood the test of time.

It had fallen into a bit of disrepair since his grandparents had moved into the new house, but Grady was enjoying the work of bringing it back to its former glory.

"I've got the old woodstove all cleaned up and set back up in the kitchen. That's going to be the hardest part, I think; trying to find someone who can cook on the old stove and help create the atmosphere of the pioneer days."

His dream wasn't just to open his bed-and-breakfast up for city people to come and spend time going on trail rides and other things you'd find on a ranch. Grady wanted something that would honor his ancestors and this property that had been in his family for years.

He wanted to give them the experience of living like the pioneers. He'd set everything up exactly how he'd pictured it to be back then, complete with lanterns and candles for the lighting and a woodstove for the cooking.

The people who came to the *Langley Pioneer B&B* were going to get the full treatment. And he already had people starting to book their vacations there, so he needed to be finished before next month.

"Well, I wish I could help, but my specialty is more on the modern appliances than on anything you'd have at the ranch. But I can't wait to see it when it's ready. It will be a wonderful addition to the Heartsbridge tourism industry."

As she went to turn and set the coffeepot on the counter behind her, Grady's eyes were drawn to the door at the back off the kitchen. He was sure he'd seen a flash of light, and a sound like air rapidly being let out of a tire.

He stood, ready to go back and help if something had gone wrong.

Moira had seen it too, and quickly turned back to face him. She reached out to place her hand on his arm, coaxing him back down to his seat.

"Oh, don't worry about that. It's just an old lamp I have back there that sometimes likes to act up." She was hustling toward the doorway, leaving him sitting there in shock.

What was she trying to hide from him? There's no way that amount of light and sound could have come from an old lamp. And if it did, she'd be wise to throw it out before it blew up her whole diner.

She quickly opened the door, and made her way through, keeping her back to him to block him from seeing inside. But as she moved to close it behind her, his eyes caught the movement of shiny blue material on a couch, and a distinct cherry-blonde head of hair struggling to sit up.

Why was Moira trying to keep anyone from seeing the woman he'd just spotted lying back there? And what had made his heart suddenly feel like it had constricted as the light had exploded in that room behind the diner?

CHAPTER 3

*C*lara's eyes scanned the horizon all around her where she sat on the hard bench out front of the small restaurant. She'd been fortunate enough to learn to read while growing up before her parents died, so she knew the sign said, "Moira's Diner." She'd never heard of a restaurant being called that, but there was so much about this time that was different from where she came from.

She repositioned herself on the bench as the clothing she wore decided to remind her just how true her thoughts were. She'd had a choice between wearing a flowery skirt or pants, like men wore. She would have preferred the skirt, but when she'd put it on, it had only come to just below her knees.

She'd never shown so much of her skin before.

So she'd opted for the pants and at least her skin would be covered. They were uncomfortable and didn't allow her to move. She almost found herself missing her corset that she'd always hated to wear. These pants weren't much better.

At least Moira had been able to give her a blouse, even if it did look like one she remembered her father wearing when she was growing up on the farm. It was plaid, and had long sleeves so she could keep the buttons done up and cover herself enough.

The loud sound of banging came from across the road where men were moving around as they worked on a building that was larger than anything she remembered seeing in her life. They all wore orange hats and vests, as they worked around equipment unlike anything she'd seen before. There were no horses moving anything around, and the men climbed into the machines and somehow just got them to go where they wanted them to.

Moira had explained a lot to her yesterday when she'd arrived, but there was just still so much she knew she'd never understand. The things Moira had called "cars" were all going past her at such fast speeds. Occasionally one would pull into the space in front and people would climb out laughing and talking as they went inside the diner. Where she'd come from, "cars" were what she'd rode on when she'd come out on the train to Texas.

How would she ever learn everything?

She still couldn't even believe any of this was true. After Cissie had told her she had a way to help her, she'd been so relieved.

But as the woman had talked, and the others at the table had listened, Clara had been sure she was sitting with people who had perhaps become feebleminded. She'd been skeptical, right up until they'd all gone into the back room of the boardinghouse and Cissie had pulled a wallet out of a locked trunk. She'd handed it to the man named Noah, and he'd opened it to show her inside.

The items in it were so different, and she wasn't sure what to make of it. Then they'd shown her something they'd called a "cell phone," and Clara had started to suspect something might be true in what they were telling her.

They'd explained how Noah and his sister

Charlotte had been from this time, and been sent back to find their heart matches. They were happy staying where they were in the past, with the people they'd found love with.

And apparently, with the hands on the watch moving, it meant she'd had a chance to do the same. Except she'd come forward, to the time they'd just come from.

Clara had been so tired, and so unsure of what her future held—she'd agreed, never honestly believing anything would happen.

When she'd woken up in Moira's back room, and had a chance to see everything around her, she'd known everything had been the truth. She was somehow now living far in the future from where she'd come from.

"I brought you some cold lemonade. You still look a bit shocked about everything, so I thought I should come and check on you."

Moira smiled down at her as she walked over with a glass of lemonade held out in her hand. Taking the frosty glass from her, Clara quickly took a sip, letting the tart liquid make its way past her lips.

"Thanks, Moira." She smiled shyly at the woman who'd been so kind to her since she'd arrived. "It's a lot to take in. I just don't know where my place will be here. I didn't have anywhere to go back home, but at least I knew I belonged there."

Moira tilted her head slightly as she kept her gaze on her. "What makes you think you belonged there? There's a reason for you being sent here, so why not just wait and see what happens? I will help you, and I'm sure in no time, you'll realize that perhaps this is actually where you do belong."

Clara moved her head as she looked around her at the people who walked past. The women were barely covered at all, and the men didn't even seem to notice anything out of the ordinary. There were no horses, and every building looked new and sturdy.

"I honestly don't know where I belong anymore." The words were out before she could stop them, and she quickly brought her hand up to cover her mouth, horrified she'd said something so private to a stranger.

Moira reached out and put her hand on her arm. "Give it a chance. I think you might end up being very happy here."

"Well, I want to pay my own way. I don't

expect you to let me stay with you without earning my keep."

Moira nodded. "I wouldn't expect anything less. Starting tomorrow, you can work at the diner with me. I can show you what you need to learn, and help you adjust to life here. And if you're still not happy after you've been here for a while, you can always go back home."

Clara's eyes caught some movement at the new building going up across the street, and turned her gaze toward it. One of the men had noticed them sitting there, and lifted his hand to wave as he carried a large bag of something on his shoulder. He was too far to see clearly, but for some reason, Clara could feel her skin heat up. It was almost as though she could see the darkness of his eyes reaching out to her.

She gave her head a quick shake and looked back at Moira who'd been watching her intently.

"That sounds perfect, Moira. Thank you. The only problem is, I don't have anything to go back home to, so I need to try and make things work here. Even if I know it's going to be hard to fit in."

They stood to go inside, but Clara could feel eyes on her and glanced back toward the man she'd seen earlier. He was standing and watching them as the other men worked around him.

Her heart racing, she quickly followed Moira back inside.

She had so much to learn about this time.

CHAPTER 4

His eyes were already searching as soon as they walked through the door to the diner. The woman he'd seen yesterday with Moira had kept him awake all night, and he couldn't quite figure out what his fascination was. It's not like she was anything like Janet, the woman he'd dated for a few years, who'd decided she needed more than Heartsbridge, and Grady could provide. Janet had been perfectly polished, with her hair never out of place and her makeup always done to highlight her beauty.

This woman seemed different somehow. She didn't need any makeup to show off the glow and purity she had radiating from her face.

He was sure she was the same woman he'd seen in the back room on the couch, and she seemed to be so lost yesterday as he'd noticed her sitting on the bench.

It was like she'd been looking around her and seeing everything for the first time.

He'd caught himself watching her the whole time she'd been outside, unable to look away. Even though he was across the parking lot, and on the other side of the street from her, his eyes had been pulled in that direction.

His heart jumped into his throat and the breath flew from his lungs when he saw her walking out from the kitchen with a pot of coffee in her hand. Her eyes were as blue as the ocean, and he could sense her wariness as the men walked in to sit down.

Moira immediately came from the kitchen and walked over with the woman. She fixed her glare on the men with Grady, letting them know she wasn't going to let them bother the new waitress.

"You can wait on him, while I take their orders." Moira nodded her head in his direction where he sat on a stool at the counter beside a couple of the other guys from the worksite.

"Oh come on, Moira, you know we'll behave." Harvey was snickering loudly, and Grady could feel the skin on the back of his neck crawl as he noticed the worry in the new girl's eyes.

Smiling widely, he reached up to take his ball cap off. "Just ignore those two. They don't have any more manners than sense." He put his hand out to her. "My name's Grady Langley. You must be new around here."

He heard a slight gasp as he said his name, but she tentatively put her hand out to his. She placed it in his facing down, as though she expected him to bring it up to his lips as he'd seen gentlemen in movies do. He clumsily took it, giving it a slight shake, and watched her face register confusion as she pulled it back.

"I'm Clara Swanson." Her eyes were locked on his. "Did you say your name was Langley?"

He nodded. "I did. My family has been in Heartsbridge for generations. Have you heard the name before?"

She swallowed hard as she continued to stare. "I believe I have." The words came out almost in a whisper as though she couldn't believe she was hearing the name. He wondered what she'd heard that was causing such disbelief. He didn't think there were any criminals or anything in his family line that would scare a woman.

Moira finished with the others and moved over to them. "Grady, this is my new waitress, Clara Swanson."

"Yes, we've met." His eyes were still trapped in the depths of blue that had him held in their grip.

Finally, Clara turned to face Moira. "His last name is Langley?" She said the words almost as a question.

Moira nodded slowly, then turned and smiled at Grady. "I assume you'll have the soup and sandwich special again today?"

Clara seemed to finally get herself together, her cheeks turning a dark shade of red as she faced him again. "I'm so sorry. I never poured you any coffee."

He fought the urge to reach out and put his hand on her arm to steady it as it shook, pouring the hot liquid into his cup. Something about his name had upset her, and she was struggling to get her composure back.

The women walked to the kitchen, and they were talking on the other side of the open window where the orders went up. He sipped his coffee as he watched, trying to see what had caused such concern.

Just then a phone rang in the back, and Moira said something to Clara before going to answer it.

Clara came through the doors and started taking the soup bowls down to set them in front of the men at the counter. He noticed she wasn't making eye contact with anyone as she went about her job.

"Hey, sweetheart, now that the old mother hen isn't around, why don't you come over here and let us introduce ourselves? We haven't seen you around town before, so how would you like us to take you out tonight and show you around Heartsbridge?"

Grady cringed as Duncan made his move on Clara. Honestly, the man had no class at all.

"No, thank you. It wouldn't be proper for me to go out with a man without an escort, especially when I don't know him."

Duncan and Harvey looked at each other, then burst out laughing. "Wouldn't be proper without an escort? Are you kidding me?"

Grady could see the confusion and embarrassment in her eyes as she backed away, her cheeks once again turning a bright red. As she turned, her eyes caught his.

"That's enough, you guys. I'm giving you fair warning right now to back off."

His voice came out low, as he struggled against the anger building inside.

They turned and faced him now. "Or what?" Harvey, the smallest of the two had the biggest mouth. Grady was sure he wouldn't be so confident without Duncan beside him.

He slowly stood, knowing that he was a tall man who would tower over them. He crossed his arms in front of him as he shrugged his shoulders. "I guess we're about to find out."

Moira came to the other side of the counter. He hadn't even noticed her coming from the kitchen. She put herself between him and the other men. "Duncan and Harvey, I've put up with you both long enough. I'm asking you to leave, and you won't be welcome back in my diner again."

"You're going to kick out paying customers?"

"I wouldn't take money from either of you now even if I never saw another customer."

The men looked around at the other people who were all watching. They probably knew their boss would get wind of what had happened, and wouldn't want to make things worse. Grady watched them go out the door, then turned and saw Clara stood with her mouth half-open.

"I'm sorry. I didn't mean to cause any problems for you." She brought her hand up to her throat.

Grady laughed as he sat back down. "Those guys cause enough problems on their own. Trust me, they aren't worth worrying over."

"Well, I for one am glad we won't be seeing them come back through those doors again." Moira was picking their cups and soup bowls up from the counter. "But I hope it won't stop you from coming back each day. You're always welcome here."

Looking past Moira, he saw the blue eyes staring back at him, and his body warmed. He knew without a doubt there was nothing that would stop him from coming back here now.

CHAPTER 5

*C*lara put the lid back on the sugar container; and smiled as she heard the familiar jingling of the door opening. It had been a few days since she'd arrived here, and she was finally starting to feel a bit more settled. Everything was taking some time to get used to, but Moira was trying her best to help her adjust.

She still had her moments though where she would realize just how different things were.

She looked up, and her heart did the familiar jump when Grady walked toward the counter. He always had a smile on his face, and had been nothing but kind to her. After she'd gotten over her initial shock of hearing the same name as the people she'd met in Cissie's boardinghouse, she was able to understand that Grady was, in fact,

Noah's great-great-grandson. Something about that thought made her feel happy to know the couple who were so in love had left a legacy in this town.

"I've got your sandwich ready, and the soup today is homemade vegetable. I made it." She was proud of her attempt today to do some of the cooking on the stove she wasn't used to. Moira had spent some time each evening after the diner closed to show her how to use the appliances.

She'd used a recipe she'd made many times over the years while working for the Dunnings. She hoped it would still taste the same even if it was using a different cooking method.

"Thanks, I can't wait to try it. I'm starving."

She laughed as she set the plate in front of him. "You always are."

He'd been in every day, even coming in on the weekends to have his lunch. Moira said he hadn't done that before, and joked that it was Clara who was bringing him in the extra days.

Moira came from the kitchen with the steaming bowl of soup. "Here you go. Clara spent all morning whipping this up."

Clara watched as he lifted the spoon to his

lips, wondering why she cared so much what he thought.

"Mmmm…this is delicious. I think you might have met your match, Moira."

He quickly took another spoonful, closing his eyes as he savored the taste. "This almost tastes like the soup my grandma would make when I was a kid. There's just something about it that makes it taste like it's an old family recipe handed down through the years." His eyes popped open and he brought his eyebrows together as he looked at Clara.

"It's too bad Moira found you before I did. I could have used someone like you to help with the bed-and-breakfast. I've never had even one reply to my ad for a house manager. I'm starting to worry there isn't anyone out there who can help me pull this off. Maybe I was crazy thinking this would be something people would find appealing."

Clara had heard him mention the bed-and-breakfast he was opening, but she hadn't realized he didn't have any help.

"When are you opening, Grady?" Moira poured him a cup of coffee.

"I was hoping to open within the next couple

of weeks. But if I can't find someone who can learn to cook with the woodstove, and to manage the house using the old methods, I don't see it being ready on time. I can't hope to make this something unique that would appeal to folks without that angle. Grandma has offered her help, but I can't expect her to do all the work. "

Clara could feel Moira's eyes on her.

"You're using a woodstove to cook for the guests?"

He shrugged as he held the sugar container over his coffee. "That was the plan. I wanted to have something different than the other B and B's around here. Give the guests the whole pioneer experience, along with trail rides and other things that would give them an enjoyable stay. I have a cousin in Montana who has a ranch bed-and-breakfast, but it's just a regular one. When I visited him a couple of years ago, I realized it was a way to help bring some life back into the ranch."

She heard the excitement in his voice as he spoke about his dream. He reminded her of how her father had been when she was a little girl. He'd always had bigger plans for the farm they had, and the life he wanted to give them.

"Well, maybe if Moira wouldn't mind, I could come out and see what I can do to help. I've actually cooked on a woodstove before, so I could help teach anyone you can find."

She surprised herself as the words tumbled from her lips. *What was she doing?* She didn't know enough about being in this time to go off with a stranger. Especially a man.

But before she could apologize for being so forward, his eyes lit up and a smile spread across his face.

"That would be wonderful. Of course, I still need to find someone who can take the job first or you won't have anyone to teach."

Moira cleared her throat and put her hand on Clara's arm. "We should get back to the kitchen to get the other orders ready."

When they got to the back, Moira turned and faced her. "Clara, you should take the job with Grady. It's something you can do to feel more connected here, and to build your own future. I'll still be here to help you, but you need to see what it is you were sent here for." Moira's glance moved to the opening where Grady was talking with the man beside him. "And I have a sneaking suspicion, the reason you're here is sitting on the other side of that counter."

Clara's eyes followed Moira's, and her chest constricted as she realized what the woman was implying. She remembered Noah and Charlotte explaining how they'd been sent back in time to find the person their hearts were meant to be with.

Was it possible Grady was that person for her?

She was scared to hope, afraid she wouldn't be able to let herself stay here when the time came to decide. What if he wasn't the right one? What if he was, but she wouldn't measure up to the women from his own time who could make him happier?

The stakes were high, but she knew she had to find out. Cissie and Moira had both told her the hands on the watch wouldn't move forever, and once they slowed down, she would need to decide if she was staying or going back.

She'd been on her own a long time now, and had to make decisions that would affect her future. But she'd never backed down from any challenge thrown her way, and had managed to survive after her parents died, leaving her alone.

Maybe it was her turn to find some happiness.

She'd come all the way to Texas to marry a stranger, so surely this wouldn't be any more difficult.

Although as the man in question turned his head to meet her eyes, giving her a smile that made her knees feel weak, she realized she might just have much more on the line this time.

CHAPTER 6

"I don't know if this is such a good idea. Are you sure this is safe?" Clara's heart was pounding as she pulled on the buckle and latched it how Moira had shown her. "I've ridden on a train before, but there are no rails or anything to hold this in place. I don't know if I'm ready for this."

Her throat was dry and her hands were clammy as she clasped them together in her lap. Since she'd arrived, she'd seen the fast-moving vehicles going past the diner, but she'd never tried riding anywhere in one until now.

"Clara, I promise, I will drive slowly. It's completely safe…well, as long as everyone around us is driving safely too."

"What do you mean by that?" Her heart sped

up even faster, which she hadn't thought was possible.

"Nothing. We'll be fine. It's not too far out to Grady's ranch. If I get going too fast for you, just tell me and I'll slow down." Moira was trying to offer her a soothing smile, but Clara was too nervous to return one.

"I guess it's a good idea for me to stay out there. I don't think I could go through this every day. And I'm sure I'll never be able to drive one myself."

Clara squeezed her eyes tight as the vehicle started to move. Her hands clung to the handle on one side, and the edge of the seat on the other as she pressed her head back. She said a silent prayer in her head, hoping she'd make it safely to Grady's.

Clara tried to take her mind off her fear, thinking about what was ahead for her, working out at the ranch and helping Grady get things ready to open. She would be in charge of cleaning the rooms and getting them set up, and making sure the kitchen was stocked with everything she needed to do the cooking once it opened.

He'd said that for now, until the B and B could bring in enough money, he'd have to continue working his construction job during the day, which meant she'd be in charge while he was gone.

Was she really ready for this?

Moira had assured her it was fine for her to be staying out at the ranch with a strange man, even if they weren't married. But since she'd still had some concerns, Grady had told her she could stay right in the room he'd been staying in at the "big house" as he called it. He'd move back in to the other house on the property with his grandparents.

She felt bad, knowing he'd prepared a room for her in the B and B she could have used, but she just didn't feel right staying in a house with a man she wasn't married to without a chaperone.

Peeking one eye open, she swallowed the fear in her throat as the landscape outside the window flew past. It was like it had been on the train when she'd come west. But she was completely relying on Moira to keep it on the road.

The ride was surprisingly smooth though, and she found herself eventually opening both eyes as she started to relax somewhat. As she looked outside, she wondered at how things seemed so much the same from where she'd come from, yet still so different. There were things she'd never seen before, mixed in with the world she was familiar with.

Horses grazed in a pasture, just like she'd seen coming on the train in her own time. Except here, they were beside this large road filled with the cars that had taken their place for travel.

In the distance, houses stood, with large buildings all around them. A lot of the houses were even bigger than some of the rich mansions in Boston. And as Moira talked and pointed things out to her, Clara realized this was considered a normal size for a house.

She thought briefly about the tiny one-room shack where she'd spent her childhood with her parents on the farm before she'd been forced to move into the city to work. She'd been so happy there, and her memories were of them always having enough to survive. It was a far cry from what the children around here would grow up in. What could you possibly need all those rooms for?

There was just so much going on all around them. She had a moment of longing for the peacefulness she hadn't even realized was there in her own time. Everyone here seemed to always be in such a hurry.

They finally slowed down and turned into a lane that led to a beautiful house in the distance. A creek ran behind the house, and the big trees that stood framing the yard made her smile, imagining how they would have been here all those years ago, with the very same people she'd met just a few days ago.

It was all so strange for her to think about.

But she didn't have time to dwell on it as Grady came out onto the porch of the house. Today he wore a cowboy hat, instead of the usual cap, and his clothes were a bit dusty. He was wiping at his pants as he came down the front steps to greet them. He came over and opened her door, offering his hand to help her out of the car.

"Sorry about the state of me. I had some cows get out, so I've spent most of the morning rounding them up and putting them back in. I didn't have time to clean up before you got here."

She was afraid her legs weren't going to hold her up after the ride she'd had here, but she took his hand and hoped she wouldn't fall flat on the ground at his feet.

Moira had already jumped out of her side and come around. She was looking up at the house.

"You've done a great job fixing this up, Grady. I've driven by here a few times over the years and always admired the beauty of the house. You've brought it back to its old glory."

Grady let go of her hand once she was standing, and looked up at the house with a smile. "I hope so. I'd like to think my ancestors who first settled here would be proud. I can only imagine the stories these walls could tell."

As they stood looking at the house, familiar sounds reached her ears. Birds called out in song, and the soothing sounds of water trickling and tumbling over the creek-bed rocks made things feel fresh and alive.

For the first time since she'd arrived in this time, Clara felt a sense of calmness surround her.

Perhaps she could learn to fit in here after all. And maybe there was a reason she felt so at peace standing where she was now.

She just hoped the hands on the watch would give her the time to find out what that reason was.

CHAPTER 7

He sat watching her as she ran her fingers along the side of the old stove. She seemed lost in thought, and he hoped she wasn't reconsidering her offer to take this job. He knew he hadn't thought everything out well, and should have had someone ready to take on the role he'd just hired her for a long time ago.

But there had never seemed to be the right person to ask, and he'd been so busy getting everything else ready, he'd put off finding anyone. It was going to be a tough job to run a household using the primitive means he had in mind. And for now, she'd have to live in it too, which meant she'd have only the basic electricity.

Knowing he still needed to provide some of

the comforts his guests would want, he'd made sure each suite was equipped with a small functioning bathroom, with shower. And since there would be bed linens, towels, and other items to wash, he'd installed a good washer and dryer off the side of the kitchen.

But there would be no Wi-Fi, no TV, or phones ringing inside the house. He wanted to make this the closest experience to the real thing he could, so when guests stayed, they would be required to put their phones in a safe in the kitchen, only to be used in emergencies. This was their chance to get back to simpler times, and escape the reality of today's life for a while.

He just hoped he could pull it off.

"This is a beautiful stove, Grady. I'm sure I'll be able to manage just fine." She turned to smile at him nervously. Moira had just left, and Clara seemed to be uncomfortable being alone with him now.

They'd spent some time walking around the property earlier, and he'd shown Clara her room. He'd been surprised when he went to get her bags and found she only had one. He cringed inwardly as he remembered the embarrassed look on her face when he'd asked where the rest of her stuff was.

"My grandparents will have dinner ready, and they've told me to make sure you know you're welcome to join us. Since we won't have any guests showing up for a few days, there isn't much for food in the big house yet."

"Oh, I hadn't thought about what I'd do for food." Her cheeks turned that familiar shade of red he'd seen so many times.

He smiled as he stood up from the chair. "Well, it's my fault. I should have made sure the house was stocked. I'll pick some things up tomorrow on my way home from work." He pushed the door in the kitchen open, and waited for her to go through.

"I feel bad leaving you out here alone during the day, but my grandparents will always be around if you need anything. You can spend the day looking around and making a list of whatever you'll need."

They made their way to the newer house on the other side of the property, around the far side of the stables. The sound of the horses whinnying as they went past filled the evening air.

"And you can always call me if you have any

questions during the day, or need me for anything."

She was quiet, looking down as they walked. Finally, she looked up and tipped her head to the side slightly. "I actually don't have a phone."

His step faltered as he stared back at her. "Why don't you have a phone?" He didn't think he knew of anyone who didn't have a cell phone. Even his grandparents had one each.

She shrugged and looked back down. "I never needed one where I came from."

As she said the words, he realized that in the week he'd known her, he'd never asked her anything about herself—where she was from, her family or anything else about her past. She'd just shown up one day, and he'd never bothered to talk to her about her life.

They reached the porch to his grandparent's house, and he wished they lived just a bit farther away so they could have had more time alone. He suddenly couldn't wait for the walk home.

The door flew open before he could say another word, and there stood his grandma grinning from ear to ear.

"And you must be, Clara. It's so nice to meet you. I'm glad Grady has found someone to help him with the cooking and cleaning of the B and B. I was starting to think I was going to have to come out of retirement and take over things down there."

His grandma took Clara by the hand and pulled her in the door, escorting her straight over to the table that was piled high with food. As always, she'd prepared a feast as though a princess would be coming for dinner.

He rolled his eyes as he sat down at his usual chair. "As if you've ever retired, Grandma. You don't know the meaning."

It was the truth. Even though his grandparents didn't run the ranch anymore, having passed on the reins to him, they still did more than they should. His grandma kept a large garden, had chickens to take care of, and was often down at the stables helping to look after the horses.

All while keeping the house full of baking and filled with food for anyone who happened to stop by to visit.

"So, where are you from, Clara? I have to say, I haven't heard such a pretty name in many years." Grady cringed as his grandpa asked the questions he should have been asking himself.

Clara gave a nervous laugh as she took a piece

of the fried chicken off the plate before passing it to him. "Thank you. I was named after my grandmother." She scooped some peas onto her plate. "I came from Boston. I worked with a family there, caring for the wife and daughter of a wealthy businessman."

Everyone at the table stopped for a brief second and looked at her. His grandma was the first to speak. "You mean, like a maid?"

He could see her eyes widen as though she thought she might have said too much. "Oh no, not really. I just helped look after the house a bit, and cared for the girl." She was obviously feeling very uncomfortable as she fiddled with the button on the neck of her blouse.

"Oh, so more like a nanny, then." His grandma nodded, obviously having decided that was exactly what she'd meant, whether it was true or not.

"Well, we're happy to have you here on the ranch, and you're welcome to make yourself at home. If there's ever anything you need, just let us know." His grandpa was talking, but Grady couldn't take his eyes off her. There was something she was hiding, or not telling the whole truth about. However, he sensed such a genuine kindness about her, he couldn't imagine what could be so awful in her past that she'd be trying to cover it up.

But he knew he was going to enjoy spending time with her while he figured it all out.

CHAPTER 8

*S*etting the bucket of soapy water on the floor, she crouched down to start on the next room. The floors in the room she'd just cleaned had been filthy, and the water had soon become as black as dirt. She had to admit, the running water was much simpler to use than it had been at the Dunnings.

Since they'd been a wealthier family, they were one of the lucky homes in Boston who'd enjoyed a running water system. However, it was nowhere near as efficient as the one in this house. The water was instantly hot, and the drain took it away to somewhere she couldn't even begin to imagine.

Her mind started to wander as she worked the warm cloth over the floor, scrubbing in the corners and as far under the bed as she could reach. She really wished she had one of her working skirts to wear, or any dress for that matter. Bending like this while wearing pants wasn't comfortable, and she felt constricted with every movement.

And she'd looked everywhere for an apron, but hadn't found anything that would work, so she was already covered with dust and grime on the front of her blouse. She'd learned to pull her hair back like Moira had shown her with the elastics, and she felt slightly free at not having to keep it pulled up tight on her head like she had back in Boston.

Of course, that had been mostly her own decision to try and keep Mr. Dunning from noticing her. When she had her hair down, he'd tried making advances.

"Oh, my dear girl, what are you doing down there?"

Clara jumped at the sound of the woman's voice. She'd been so caught up in her thoughts, rubbing the floorboards down, she hadn't even heard anyone come into the house or up the stairs.

She quickly stood, wiping down the front of

her blouse as she faced Grady's grandmother standing in the doorway. "Mrs. Langley, I didn't even hear you come in." Her hand came up to her chest as she tried to calm her still racing pulse.

"I'm sorry, child, I didn't mean to startle you. I just didn't expect to see you on your hands and knees scrubbing the floors like Cinderella. I'm sure Grady has a good mop you could be using."

Clara immediately realized she'd once again inadvertently done something that must not be the normal manner in this time anymore. She'd always washed floors by hand, never having found any of the mops in her day to be of any use. But she should have realized things would be much more improved in this time.

"Oh, I know. I just prefer to really give floors a good, firm clean once in a while. I want everything to be perfect for the opening." She tried to brush it off and hoped the woman wouldn't see the embarrassment she was feeling.

"Well, you come downstairs with me. I brought you something to eat. It isn't much, but I figured you'd be hungry, and might be apt to think you'd be imposing by coming up to the house for lunch."

Clara smiled at the woman. She'd somehow

known exactly how Clara would be feeling, even if she hadn't wanted to admit it herself. Her stomach grumbled as though to give away how true the words were.

"I can't believe that grandson of mine would be so inconsiderate as to drag you all the way out here to start getting things cleaned up and ready, without making sure he had the cupboards stocked up first. Honestly, I don't know where his head is sometimes."

Clara couldn't help the small laugh that escaped. "It's fine, Mrs. Langley. Honestly, he's been so busy; and I'm just glad he's given me the chance to do this job. I think it will be perfect for me."

"Please, call me Anne. Mrs. Langley makes me sound old."

The woman was busy pulling sandwiches, fruit, cookies, and cake out of the bag she'd brought down. She reached back in and pulled out some strange looking items that looked like cups with lids.

"I grabbed a couple of cold Cokes to bring down for you too."

Clara eyed them warily, unsure how she was supposed to open them. Moira had told her about

Coke and other soft drinks while she'd worked at the diner, but they'd been poured from a machine. She'd never tried any of them because they looked so foamy, she wasn't sure they'd taste very good at all.

Anne set everything out and was sitting at the table, waiting for Clara to join her. "Do you not like Coke? I'm sorry, I don't know what I was thinking. I suppose not everyone likes the taste."

Clara felt guilty that the woman had gone to such trouble for her. She didn't want to make her feel bad about bringing a drink just because Clara wasn't sure how to even open it. "No, it's fine. I was just shocked at how much food you brought. I thought you said you hadn't brought much...I think you've got enough here to feed a family of ten." She laughed softly as she sat down across from Anne.

Clara kept her eyes on Anne as she picked up the Coke and pushed her fingernails in under the metal ring at the top. When she lifted it, Clara heard a loud pop and hiss. When it did that, she pulled it back then lifted the drink up to her lips.

Taking one of the sandwiches off the plate, Clara decided she'd wait until Anne was talking before she'd try opening her own. Hopefully if she had any trouble, it wouldn't be noticed.

Anne was a lovely woman, and as she started to talk, Clara realized where Grady had gotten his manners and kindness from. He'd been raised to be a gentleman, and it was obvious Anne had been a guiding hand in that.

She slowly reached out while Anne was telling Clara about the history of the house they were in, and put her hands around the drink. She tried to push her fingers under the ring like she'd seen Anne do, but nothing seemed to move. When she looked down, she couldn't figure it out. Perhaps she was trying to push on the wrong side of it.

She moved her fingers to the other side, and felt it move slightly, so she pushed them in all the way until she heard a slight hiss. It hadn't popped like Anne's had, but it seemed like it was starting to open.

"Are you all right, Clara?" Anne reached across the table and took the drink from her, easily popping the top open before handing it back. Clara could feel her hands trembling as she fought against the embarrassment of once again looking foolish.

Swallowing hard, she pasted a smile on her

face. "Yes, I guess my hands are just a bit tired from scrubbing so hard on the floors."

Anne studied her for what seemed like hours, before slowly nodding. Clara brought the drink up to her lips and took a sip, desperate to soothe the dry throat she was fighting against.

As she took the first sip, the sensation of the liquid on her lips startled her, and she ended up taking more in than she'd wanted. She started to choke, sputtering and coughing against the burning in her throat.

This wasn't refreshing in the least, and she was sure there was something wrong as it started to bubble against the back of her mouth.

Anne ran to the sink and poured some water into a glass, rushing back to push it into Clara's hands. "Here, take a sip."

Clara drank the soothing water quickly, hoping to get rid of the awful taste that had been left from the bubbly liquid. She couldn't even bring herself to lift her eyes to face the woman standing beside the table.

What must she be thinking?

"Well, Clara, my dear. If I didn't know better, I'd say you'd never seen a Coke before in your life."

Something in the way she said it made Clara look up at her. *Did she suspect something?*

"But that wouldn't be possible, would it?" Anne laughed slightly, then went and sat back down across from her, talking again like nothing had happened. However, there was something now in the way she watched her.

Clara was going to have to work harder at fitting in. Maybe she should go back to Moira's until she'd been here long enough to learn everything she'd need to know about this time period.

But that meant she'd have to leave Grady, and that wasn't something she was prepared to do yet. If he was the reason she'd been sent here, she was determined to find out.

Even if she had to make a complete fool of herself to get there.

CHAPTER 9

*H*e pushed the front door open, and called out to Clara. He'd taken the day off work to do the last-minute jobs to ready everything for their first guests who were booked in tomorrow. People from town were coming out for tours, and he even had the local paper doing an interview for opening day.

He'd talked with Clara, and she'd agreed to wear period costumes for the grand opening. In fact, she'd said she'd be fine wearing them all the time when guests came, but he'd said that was something they could decide later. She'd told him to talk to Moira about possibly finding something she could wear. And he'd brought a box of clothing back she had stored in the diner's back room. He couldn't believe the luck that she'd have something that fitted Clara with such short notice.

"Clara? Where are you?"

They'd been working together for the past few days in the evenings when he'd gotten home from work. Now that she seemed to be over her initial shyness around him, he was starting to see her true personality shining through. When she laughed, her eyes completely lit up the room. She'd shared some stories about growing up on a farm outside of Boston, but she never really gave many details. It appeared as though she'd had a simple upbringing, which could explain why she seemed content with anything she had.

She never complained, and was always genuinely happy to just be around the ranch. He figured by now she'd be asking to get a ride into town for some shopping, or ask to borrow a vehicle to go herself, but she just spent her days cleaning and preparing the house.

He came around the corner into the kitchen, and Clara stood near the doorway into the laundry room. There were soap bubbles all over the floor, and she was standing looking at him like a deer caught in the headlights. He stood in shock, trying to figure out where to start fixing the mess. First things first—try to get to the washing machine and shut it off where more water and soap poured over the top. Then grab a mop and bucket to clean up the water already on the floor.

His eyes met Clara's and the wetness of tears had left a trail down her cheeks. In that moment, he didn't even care about the mess on the floor. He walked straight over to her and without thinking, put his hand out to pull her into his arms.

"Clara, it's no big deal. We can clean this all up." He needed to let her know he wasn't upset, because the look on her face left no doubt she was afraid of what he was going to say.

"I'm so sorry. I tried to do what I'd seen Moira do when I stayed with her, but I couldn't figure out how to work it right. Now I've made a mess, and the bedding isn't even going to be ready in time for tomorrow."

She wasn't making any sense as she rambled on about what she'd done.

He pulled back and reached his hand out to lift her chin so she'd have to look at him. "Clara, we can get this cleaned up and the bedding dry before tomorrow. It's not like we need to hang it all outside. We'll just use the dryer." She'd had him set up a clothesline outside so she could hang things to dry, saying it would be a nice touch to have the linens freshly hung, and smelling of fresh air.

Her chin trembled as she struggled to regain control of her emotions. "I don't know if I'm really the person you should be leaving in charge of keeping things running around here. I just don't know what I'm doing."

He laughed softly. "Honestly, you have no idea how much you've helped. Your ideas for making everything seem true to the time period, and your willingness to work at this tirelessly to get everything ready, have been a huge help. Grandma told me you'd even washed all the floors in the entire house by hand. So don't tell me you aren't the right person to do this job."

She stepped back out of his arms, and he immediately wanted to pull her back. He missed her warmth, and he realized with a sudden lurch in his stomach that he'd started to truly care for the woman in front of him. She was so unlike the women around here. It was like she brought a breath of fresh air into a room when she entered.

But he knew he'd have to tread lightly so he didn't scare her away.

"Let's grab a couple of buckets and mops,

and we'll get this cleaned up. Then I think we need to take some time off this afternoon to relax before tomorrow." He turned to pull the dial on the washing machine and stop the cascade of water but as he stepped toward it, his feet slipped out from under him on the wet floor.

He went down hard, banging his elbow on the side of the doorway.

Clara gasped and moved to help him, but instead she fell directly on top of him. Her elbow managed to find his ribs, and he let out a whoosh of air as he winced in pain.

His eyes had squeezed shut as she landed, and when he finally opened them, he was met with the striking blueness staring at him in utter horror over what had happened. Neither of them moved as the shock of the situation settled in. Finally, he was surprised to see the corners of her lips start to turn up. She bit her lip and fought against the laughter he could see was starting to well up inside her.

"I would say I'm sorry, again. But honestly, if you could have seen the look on your face..." Now, she did start to laugh. His pride would be seriously wounded if not for the fact that her laughter had lit up her entire face, and erased the embarrassment he'd seen there before.

If it made her feel better, he'd deal with his wounded ego later.

"I'm quite sure you've managed to break my ribs, but hopefully I can still help you clean this mess up. Of course, you're going to have to get off me first." He really didn't want to make her move, but the truth was, her elbow was still digging into his stomach and as much as he liked having her close, getting rid of the pain won out.

She pushed herself up, then carefully held onto the side of the doorway to pull herself up. He stood too and shook soap suds off his now soaked hands.

She was still chewing on the corner of her lip, trying to keep from laughing.

Smiling to himself, he carefully turned to shut the washing machine off. She could laugh all she wanted if it meant he'd get to see the joy he was seeing in her eyes at this moment.

CHAPTER 10

The air touched her face, gently blowing her hair back as the horse walked along the trail through the trees. It had been so long since she'd been able to ride, and it felt so good to feel the strength of the animal move beneath her.

She let her eyes close as she tipped her face up to the sunlight, letting herself enjoy the freedom and fresh air. Since she'd arrived in this time, she'd been unable to just get away and do something for herself without being dependent on someone else.

Her eyes opened again and she turned to see the man who was riding alongside her. Her heart lurched as she realized he was watching her with a smile on his face. She hoped she wasn't doing anything that wasn't proper. Maybe women weren't supposed to enjoy riding so much.

"It's been a while since I've been able to get up on a horse. When I grew up on the farm, I had my own pony I used to ride everywhere. After I started working in Boston, we didn't get to ride the horses much anymore, being taken everywhere with carriages..." She quickly stopped and covered her mouth. "Oops, I mean the cars."

She needed to change the subject before he had time to think about it. "It's really beautiful here. You're lucky to have been able to grow up on this ranch."

His eyebrows had come together briefly, until she mentioned the ranch. As soon as she did, his face lit up with the pride of talking about the land his family owned. His eyes moved around the horizon as they made their way along the path. The only sounds she could hear were the hooves hitting the ground, and the squeaking of the saddles as they moved. Now and then, a bird would call out in the trees they passed, singing a song that filled the surrounding air.

"I am lucky. There's no better place than being out here on a horse, and working under the open sky."

She watched him for a moment as he looked all around.

"So, why don't you ranch full-time? Surely you don't need to keep doing the work you've been doing in town."

"The past few years have been tough on the economy around here. Our ranch was hit hard, and I've tried to keep things going the best I could. That's why I hope the B and B can help breathe some new life into things, and maybe give me the money I need to keep the ranch running. I had to take the construction job to help pay the bills while I built the old house back into what it is now."

He turned and smiled at her. "But hopefully that's something I can give up soon. Then I can spend my days back here, doing what I love. Of course, that's if you're willing to stay and make sure the B and B is running smoothly too."

She was surprised he still wanted her to stay after the washing machine incident this morning. She still struggled with so many things she was trying to learn, and worried that eventually he'd see she wasn't able to do what he needed.

He stopped his horse next to a big tree with the creek that ran through the property trickling past. He threw his leg over and hopped down to the ground, then reached his hand up to take her reins while she dismounted. He led the horses to the cold water and reached into the bag he'd thrown over the saddle.

"We can sit here and have some sandwiches Grandma whipped up for us. She said to let you know she's only sent some nice cold water to drink because she knows how much you don't like Coke."

She cringed, remembering the day she'd spat the Coke across the table as she sputtered and choked in front of Anne.

"That will be perfect."

He handed her a blanket, then walked over to the tree and set the food on the ground. He took the blanket from her and snapped it out, spreading it out beneath the shade of the tree.

"It's been a while since I've been on a picnic. I don't think I've done this since I was a kid with my grandma." He plopped down onto the blanket and unwrapped a sandwich. She stood awkwardly looking down at him, unsure if it was proper for her to be out here like this with him in so intimate a setting.

And she wasn't sure how to sit ladylike while

wearing these pants. They were so tight, she was sure she'd never be able to bend. The proper thing would be for him to help her sit down, but he was already biting into his sandwich.

Finally, after standing there for a few moments, he looked up at her. He was slowly chewing the bite he'd just taken. His eyebrows came together as he raised one hand up toward her. "Are you all right?"

She took his hand and kneeled down beside him, praying her pants wouldn't rip as she placed her ankles underneath herself. When she was seated, she let go of his hand and worked at brushing the imaginary wrinkles out of the skirt she wasn't wearing.

When she was sure he wouldn't be looking at her anymore, she lifted her head back up. Her breath caught in her throat as their eyes met. He was watching her so intently, she instantly felt heat rise to her cheeks.

"My legs were just a bit stiff, I was worried I'd fall on top of you again." It wasn't completely a lie. And just because they did things a bit different here, there was no reason why a man shouldn't offer his hand to help a woman sit down anyway.

She pretended not to be bothered at all, and

reached out to pick up a sandwich for herself. She smiled sweetly at him as she bit into it, letting the taste of the ham and fresh bread take over. It had been a few hours since she'd had breakfast, so she was hungry enough to be able to ignore the way he was still watching her.

When he finally looked away, she let go of the breath she'd been holding. What was it about the way he looked at her that seemed to get her stomach in a knot?

Was this what falling in love was supposed to feel like?

The words hit her like a bolt of lightning. *Was* she falling in love? Or was she still just waiting to see if Grady was the one she was sent here to find?

As he turned and handed her a bottle of water, with the lopsided smile that showed his dimple, she realized it might just be both.

CHAPTER 11

He knew they really should be getting back, but this was the first time he'd been able to relax in so long, he hated to leave. Spending the afternoon with Clara out here had been exactly what they both needed. It had taken her a while, but she'd eventually loosened up a bit and had opened up to him more.

They'd talked about their lives growing up, and spoke of the difficulties they both faced when they lost their parents. But no matter what she told him, he always felt like she was holding more back. Sometimes she'd start to say something and catch herself, often changing the subject or turning the conversation back to him.

"I love listening to you speak about your family and the history you have here on this land.

It makes me long to have something like that for myself. A place to call home."

He watched her as she spoke, a smile on her face as her eyes moved around the countryside where they sat. The gentle babble of water sounded from the creek as it wound its way along the rocks. Now and then, one of the horses would snort loudly and shake it's head, breaking the peacefulness of the world around them. She sat with her legs still under her, and off to the side slightly so she could lean on one arm.

She was beautiful. As usual, she wasn't wearing any makeup, and her hair was worn pulled back at the top and held with an old-fashioned barrette.

She wore denim pants and one of the few blouses he'd seen her wear. Now that he thought about it, he'd never seen her in a regular T-shirt or anything other than a blouse with the sleeves pulled down and buttoned right to the top.

There was something intriguing about her; and how she didn't feel the need to flaunt her beauty in front of him.

His mind briefly fluttered to Janet and how obsessed she'd been with wearing only the fanciest and newest trends, her hair always perfectly colored and styled, nails manicured regularly and full face of makeup. She would never have spent an afternoon sitting on top of a horse, then out in the open like this. She hated being outdoors altogether.

They'd dated since high school, when he'd let his hormones decide what he thought he wanted in a woman. As they'd gotten older, she became comfortable and he'd never realized how high-maintenance she really was until she'd left.

Now, sitting across from this woman who was like a breath of fresh air, he realized how imma-ture he'd been to believe that was what he wanted in a partner. He fought the urge to reach out and pull her to him, not sure if she would welcome it or not.

"Did I ever tell you about the stories that have been passed down in our family about my first ancestors to settle this land in Heartsbridge?" He wasn't ready for their time alone to end; hopefully this topic would buy him some more time out here with her.

"Stories about what?" She turned to give him her full attention. With Clara, she always listened completely. She still didn't have a cell phone, so when anyone spoke to her, she wasn't looking down at her phone and texting, or trying to talk over them with her own stories.

"Well, over the years, there have been a few strange tales passed down through the family mentioning some of my ancestors from way back. There has been mention of true love stories, like with my great-great-grandfather Noah and his wife Elizabeth. There have been hints that Noah Langley couldn't have been from his time, and must have time-traveled to be with his true love."

Clara had been taking a sip of her water, with her eyes wide as she listened. As soon as he mentioned the story about Noah Langley, she spat her water out and started coughing loudly. She jumped up from her spot on the blanket and bent over as she tried to catch her breath.

He hopped up and went over to make sure she was all right. Grady patted her back as she sputtered and he wiped at the water droplets running down his cheek that had ended up on him.

"Are you okay?" He didn't know what to do to help her as she gasped for air, holding her hand on her chest.

"Yes, I'm fine. I just swallowed my water wrong." She tried to talk, but her voice came out in broken wheezes between coughing fits.

After a few moments, she finally managed to get her breathing under control. She lifted her eyes and gave him a weak smile.

"Sorry, I didn't mean to soak you with water. I'm not sure what got into me."

Her cheeks were red, but this time he couldn't tell if it was from embarrassment or the exertion of her choking fit. He figured it was likely a little of both.

"Maybe it was the talk about time-travel." He laughed, trying to lighten the mood.

Her eyes went bigger again, and he saw her swallow. "Maybe. It's kind of a strange thing to bring up."

He shrugged. "I guess. It's just a part of our family stories that have made their way through the generations. I know it's crazy, but some of the others have speculated and tried to uncover what they think could have been possible."

She was watching him closely. "And what do you believe?"

He wasn't about to admit to her he was one of the few who had really questioned the stories he'd heard over the years, and had wondered if there could somehow be some truth to it.

Obviously from her reaction, she would think

he was unhinged for putting any thought into any truth behind those stories.

He chuckled loudly. "Oh, I don't believe it. I mean, it's all very romantic and makes for some fun stories around the Christmas tree, but the thought that Noah had somehow gone back in time to find Elizabeth is a bit much to believe."

She stood stock-still in front of him, but her shoulders still moved fast as she tried to bring her breathing back under control. "Why do people believe he'd traveled in time anyway?"

"Well, it wasn't just him. Apparently he had a sister too, named Charlotte, who has been mentioned too. The stories started way back, about how they just showed up in town, and no one really knew where they came from. Then, over the years, I suspect the stories just grew from there." He watched her warily. Should he mention the clues that had been found?

"My grandpa talks about Noah, his grandfather, quite a bit. He always tells me how much I remind him of him, and how my eyes are the spitting image of his. I've seen pictures, and I do actually look a lot like him. He's always talked of how obvious his grandparent's love was for each other. And a couple of times, he said his grandpa would "slip" and say something about a time that hadn't happened yet. Apparently he didn't think much about it as a kid, but as he got older and some of the things started to happen, he thought back and remembered his grandpa saying these things."

Clara still hadn't moved a muscle, obviously enthralled in the story.

"And there's an old dollar bill that looks like it's been around for centuries, that's been held in our family safe. It's been said it came from under a rock that was near an old dugout on the property, as though it had been dropped and never noticed. But the bill wasn't one that would have been around in his time. It's a bill from now."

As he usually did when talking about this, he found himself getting more excited. It was a story he'd always loved to think about, and imagine as though it could have happened.

"Then, and I haven't ever told anyone about this yet—even my grandparents—I found something when I was working on the house. When I got down to the studs in the original space where the old cabin had stood, I found a piece of paper tucked in behind one of the boards. It was a note, signed by my great-great-grandfather, Noah Langley."

"What did it say?" Her words were softly whispered, and he could see she was caught up in the story just as much as he was.

"It said, *Don't let her go. Love will find a way, and even time itself can't keep you apart if your hearts are meant to be together.*"

CHAPTER 12

*S*he sat in the quiet of the night, with the glow of the moon highlighting the shadows around her. She had a small lantern she'd carried outside, which gave off a flickering light that kept the darkness at bay. There was a yard light up by the other house, and her eyes were held there, knowing Grady was asleep inside.

The day alone with him had been perfect, until the moment he'd mentioned the story about Noah Langley. She cringed as she remembered how she'd reacted. Spitting water all over poor Grady's face as he tried to share a story from his family's past. Groaning to herself, she had to shake her head at what he must be thinking about her by now.

First, she exploded water all over the house

when attempting to do laundry. Then, he'd slipped in the mess and she'd ended up landing on top of him, almost breaking his ribs. As if that wasn't enough for one day, she'd spat her drink across at him, leaving him soaked.

Who was she kidding by thinking she could stay here in this time?

Although she loved being here on this ranch, and with Grady, she wasn't sure where his feelings were headed. And she couldn't stay here if he wasn't going to return them. Somehow, she'd managed to let herself fall for him, so she knew now without a doubt he was the reason she'd been sent here.

But she couldn't force someone to fall in love with her.

And the way she'd acted today had likely hurt any chance she might have had of that happening.

Why would Noah have left that note? Was it her he was talking about, leaving it for Grady to find? Did that mean she'd be leaving?

It didn't make sense. Of course, not much had made sense to her since stepping off that stage-coach in Heartsbridge.

"Shouldn't you be getting rested up for tomorrow? It's likely going to be a long day."

She jumped as Grady's voice reached out in the darkness. He came around the front and into the subtle glow of the lantern.

"You know, when you're here by yourself, you can use the electricity and turn some outside lights on. I don't like you being here all by yourself in the dark." He came and sat down on the step in front of her, turning slightly to face her and lean back on the porch railing.

"I'm not scared of the dark. I grew up with it like this, so it's not really anything different for me. Besides, it's not like you're that far away."

"You didn't have electricity when you were growing up?" He sounded surprised, and she realized she was so tired of having to watch everything she said around him. But he'd said himself he didn't believe the time-travel stories, and she hated to think he wouldn't be able to believe her either.

"Well, we did, but since we didn't have much money, we used it sparingly." She hated to keep lying like this. She felt like every lie she told just took her further away from him.

He sat watching her for what seemed like an

eternity, before he reached his hand out and took hers. "Clara, I just wanted to thank you for coming out to help me with all of this. I couldn't have done it without you."

Her heart pounded so hard she was sure even the horses in the far pen would be able to hear every beat. She knew she shouldn't be sitting out here alone like this with a man, but her legs wouldn't move.

All around them, the sounds of the night started to fade into the background. The flickering light reflected in his face, and she could see his eyes staring into hers.

"And before the rush of everything starts to happen tomorrow, I need to tell you something else." His voice was low as he spoke, and he continued to hold her hand. She was sure she'd stopped breathing as she waited to hear what else he would say.

"Since the day I first saw you sitting on that bench outside of Moira's Diner, I haven't been able to stop thinking about you. I don't know what it is, but there's something that pulls me to you, and it's making me crazy. But the last thing I want to do is scare you away. I need to know if you're feeling anything too."

She'd never had a man look at her the way Grady was right now. The words hung in the air between them as he gently moved his thumb on the back of her hand.

She couldn't find her voice, so all she did was nod. It was all he needed, and before she knew what was happening, he'd moved up beside her and was pulling her to him. His lips met hers with a burst of heat that shot through her entire body.

As he slowly moved them on hers, his other hand tangled in her hair. He caressed the skin on the back of her neck, leaving a trail of fire everywhere he touched.

If she'd ever doubted that he was truly who she'd been sent here for, she was left with no question in her heart now.

$\sim$

THE FIRST GUESTS had called and said they would be here by mid-morning. It was a group of adult friends from New York who were taking a road trip across the states and taking in as much history and sights as they could do in a month. They were excited to spend a couple of days living like pioneers, and spending time in the outdoors on some trail rides around the property.

The newspaper from town was coming out after lunch to do a story on the new business in town, and to get some thoughts from the guests on their first impressions of the Langley Pioneer B&B.

Grady tried to keep his stomach from churning with worry, but the truth was, he'd hardly slept a wink last night and he was paying for it today. He wasn't sure if it had been the thoughts about the opening that kept him awake, or the deep blue eyes and soft lips that were haunting his thoughts.

He smiled at the familiar warm feeling that snaked its way through his insides as he thought about Clara. The kiss they'd shared last night had left him breathless. She was so innocent and as he'd held her in his arms, he was sure he'd never felt more complete.

And now today, he was about to see his dream come true for the ranch. He hoped Clara coming into his life at this moment was a sign that every-thing was going to work out, and the ranch would be able to thrive like it had before.

He hopped up the steps of the front porch,

excited to see Clara after the moment they'd shared last night. He couldn't remember ever feeling this eager to see a woman before. Considering he'd only ever dated Janet, he could understand it. Clara was like seeing the sun after years of night.

As he rounded the corner into the kitchen, he saw his grandma had already beaten him here.

"Hey, Grandma, how did I know you'd be here bright and early helping Clara?"

She turned from the cupboard and gave him a curtsy in the dress she'd pulled out to wear. She had it from years ago when they'd celebrated the centennial for Heartsbridge and everyone had dressed up in pioneer clothes.

"I even pulled out my old bonnet, which I'll put on once the guests arrive." She was grinning and Grady was glad to see her this excited about something.

"Where's Gramps?"

"Oh, he's already out in the stables getting the horses brushed down and looking their best he says. I haven't seen him so enthusiastic about anything in a long time, so I hope he won't get under your feet too much as you get things going around here."

He knew that could never happen. There wasn't a man in the world he admired more than his grandpa, so if he wanted to get his hands dirty once in a while and help out, Grady would welcome the company.

His eyes were moving around the kitchen to look down the hall toward the stairs that led up to Clara's room.

"Are you looking for someone else?" His grandma's eyes twinkled with mischief.

Raising his eyebrow, he shook his head at his grandma. "I think you know who I'm looking for."

She leaned back against the counter, tipping her head to the side. "I haven't seen you this smitten with a woman before."

He laughed. "Smitten, Grandma? Really? Just because we're pretending to be from the old west, doesn't mean we need to talk like that when it's just the two of us."

"You never mind, Grady Langley. Don't tease your old grandma."

They were so busy talking, he hadn't even noticed Clara come down the stairs. When she walked into the room, the world around him seemed to stop. He wasn't sure if he was breathing or not as he watched her float into the room. She was smiling at him, with a hint of uncertainty in her eyes. He didn't know if it was because of their kiss or because she wasn't sure how he'd react to seeing her wearing the period dress.

His eyes moved down her dress to take it all in. She was absolutely breathtaking. And she looked like she'd been born to wear that dress.

Suddenly, his heart lurched as he realized he'd seen that fabric before.

"It *was* you on the couch that day, wearing this dress in Moira's back room at the diner."

CHAPTER 13

She stared at him in disbelief for a moment, trying to figure out what to say. Whatever she said was going to be just one more lie, and it tore her apart to have to do it. This wasn't how she wanted to start things with him.

But this wasn't the time or place to try explaining the truth to him. She could do that later.

Her eyes darted to where Anne stood watching them closely. Her eyebrows were pulled together like she'd seen Grady do so many times as he concentrated on something. When their eyes met, Anne gave her an encouraging smile.

"Oh, this dress? Yes, you might have seen me with it on that day in the back room. It's Moira's and she was trying to get it hemmed up. She asked me to put it on so she could take it up enough." She knew the answer she was giving him sounded completely unreasonable, but she couldn't think fast enough to know what else to say.

Luckily, Anne must have noticed something was up, so she stepped forward and took her arm. "You look perfect. Like you stepped right out of the nineteenth century. Of course, most pioneer women wouldn't have had a dress quite so fashionable, but it's perfect for opening day, isn't it Grady?"

Anne gave her grandson a stern look, forcing him to acknowledge how good she looked. But she could see he still knew she was hiding something.

The dress she wore was the one she'd arrived in. Little did Anne know, most of the dresses she'd worn herself back in her own time *were* more like the ones worn by the women on the wild frontier. She didn't own any fancy dresses like this one.

But when Mrs. Dunning had found out she was going west to get married, she'd insisted Clara take a couple of dresses of her daughter's that she didn't wear anymore.

This one was her favorite. It was one she'd

always admired when Constance Dunning, the spoiled daughter who'd been Clara's own age, had worn it. The soft blueish-green color of the fabric was beautiful, and Clara had planned to wear it when she'd married Martin. Since she'd soon realized that wasn't going to happen, she'd put it on that day when she woke up at Cissie's.

She'd figured just because she wasn't going to get married, it didn't mean she should never get the chance to wear that dress.

"We better get to work. I thought it would be wonderful to have the smell of fresh bread in the woodstove when the guests arrive." She avoided looking at Grady as she moved over toward the stove.

"I've already got it all stoked up and ready, so Grady, you can go help your grandfather while Clara and I look after things here."

Clara had to fight back the smile as she caught the surprised look on Grady's face. He knew he'd just been dismissed by his grandma.

But before he left, he caught her eye and smiled at her. Her heart soared, knowing that even though he suspected she wasn't telling him everything, he wasn't just going to walk away from her.

She promised herself she would find the time to try and tell him everything. If he couldn't believe her, hopefully he would at least still be willing to give them a chance. She knew it would be hard if he looked at her differently, and if he didn't believe, but she couldn't keep up with the lies any more.

Tonight, once they'd gotten through the excitement of the first day, she'd sit down and talk with him.

"You look lovely, dear. You truly look like you were meant to be wearing that dress. I'm glad you're getting the chance to wear it for this. It would be a shame to have it sitting and collecting dust." Anne was pulling some of the bowls down and getting the ingredients they'd need for the bread.

She was such a kind woman, and someone Clara had grown quite fond of since she'd been here. It was going to make things easier to have her working alongside her today, and even a bit more fun.

"Thanks for helping with everything today, Anne. I was a bit nervous I wouldn't be able to pull everything off once the guests arrived. I'm more of a person who prefers to stay in the background where people can't notice me, than being out in the public eye. So I appreciate having you here." Clara grabbed an apron and got to work.

"Well, Grady has put his heart into bringing this old house back into something that might be able to help save the ranch. It breaks my heart to think there would ever be any chance of us losing the land that has been in my husband's family for so many years. I want nothing more than for everything Grady has worked so hard for to become a success." Anne lifted her eyes and smiled at her.

"And I want him to also be happy. Which I can see he is when you're around."

Anne was watching her carefully, so she looked back down at the dough she was starting to put together, hoping the woman wouldn't notice how much her cheeks were burning.

"Don't ever let your worries about how someone else will see you, or what they will believe once they know all of your truths stop you from letting them know what's in your heart. If two hearts are truly meant to be together, love will help them find a way."

Clara quickly turned her head to look at

Anne, who was now smiling to herself as she rolled out her dough.

Why was Grady's grandma saying that to her? How could she possibly have known what she was feeling?

They worked together to get the dough finished and the bread in the oven, just in time for Grady to come in the door to let them know their first guests were pulling up outside.

There were two couples, and a single friend, who were registered to stay. At least it wasn't a large group for their first guests. Clara was suddenly starting to feel like her heart was in her throat as she walked out to greet them on the front porch.

She hadn't even noticed Grady had worn old-looking pants with suspenders over his work shirt, along with his cowboy hat. He looked every bit the old rancher from days gone by.

He put his hand out for her and walked her down the steps to the car that was coming to a stop.

His grandparents stood beside them, and Clara could feel the pride radiating from them both.

The crunching of the gravel under the tires

stopped, and the engine shut off. As the doors started to open, Clara smiled at the man and woman who'd just stepped out of the car. The back door was thrown open, and another woman jumped out.

"Grady!"

She ran over and flung herself at him, forcing him to let go of Clara's hand to steady himself from falling. The woman was kissing him all over both of his cheeks.

Clara stood helplessly watching as the beautiful woman with long black hair told Grady how much she'd missed him. She was exactly the kind of woman who belonged in this time, with her hair perfectly done and wearing the clothes that showed off every curve she had.

Struggling to keep the smile on her face, she turned her eyes to Grady's face, fearing what she would see.

He was looking at this new woman in his arms, and Clara realized at that moment, she was so different from the women of this time that she could never hope to figure out how to be like them.

Her eyes fell down to her dress with long sleeves, flowing all the way to the ground, covering every square inch of skin on her body. This was what she was comfortable wearing.

The woman in front of her wore a dress that barely covered her backside, and had only little straps holding it up. It was something Clara knew she could never wear, even if she stayed in this time for the rest of her life.

Grady deserved someone who could make him happy, and who would be able to fit in with the world he belonged in. Someone who understood how the world worked now.

And that someone could never be her.

CHAPTER 14

"I always knew you'd make this place into something big. What a wonderful idea you had to turn it into a B and B. Now you just need to get the word out there, start spreading it on social media and building up some buzz about it."

Janet's voice seemed to control the conversation of everyone around the table. They'd all insisted Grady join them for lunch since he was an old friend of Janet's, even though it wasn't something he planned to do with the guests regularly. But since the newspaper would be here soon, he needed to make sure everyone stayed happy enough to help give a good report.

Inside though, his stomach was in turmoil. He was having a hard time swallowing, his eyes finding their way to Clara every time she came in the room. But she never made eye contact with him when she came in to set something on the table, or to clear anything off. The dining area was just off the kitchen, and every now and then she'd walk past the open doorway as she went about making sure the meal was perfect.

He'd seen the sadness in her face when Janet had thrown herself at him. If he hadn't been so shocked, he'd have immediately pushed the woman away, instead of letting her shower him with kisses and wrapping her entire body around his.

By the time he'd gotten his senses back under control, he'd set Janet away from him and turned to Clara. But it had been too late. Her face still held a smile, but there was no mistaking the hurt in her eyes. Everything was still so new and unsure between them, and to see a scantily-dressed woman in his arms had obviously stung. Especially for a woman like Clara, who was so much more reserved and old-fashioned.

He would explain to her tonight that there was nothing at all between him and Janet anymore, even if the woman was making sure everyone around them thought there still was.

"When I first heard what you were doing, I couldn't wait to let my friends know so we could be sure to stop in on our planned trip. You should definitely sit down and talk with Davis here. He's the top marketer in his firm, and honestly would be able to put your little B and B on the map. You'd have people coming here in droves."

As much as he wanted the B and B to be successful, the thought of people descending here in droves made his stomach sink. He wanted to do well with it, but he also didn't want it to turn into some big attraction that took away from the down-home, pioneer feel he was hoping to achieve.

The man named Davis nodded his head. "Yes, you're sitting on a gold mine here. People are looking for places to get away and shut off from the world around them. This is the perfect little paradise."

"Well, I hope to become a tourist destination, but I also don't want to get too big, too fast. There's just me and Clara, as well as my grand-parents at the moment, working it. We want to keep the homey feel to it."

"Oh, well, Grady, this is where you're in luck. I've decided to move back home to Heartsbridge.

I'll help with all the marketing I've learned from Davis, and can handle all the bookings. I know how much you hate doing that kind of thing, so you can hand it all off to me."

Clara had just walked back in with the dessert plates, and her step faltered as Janet spoke.

Her eyes finally met his, and he was sure he saw a hint of anger in them. In all the time he'd known her, he didn't remember ever seeing her mad.

"I appreciate your offer, Janet. But at the moment we have enough of us working here. If I was looking for any help, it would be more for Clara so she isn't having to spend every day cleaning up after guests and making the meals. Grandma is helping at the moment, but they could both use time off now and then."

Janet brought her hand up to her chest, showing off her flawless red manicure. She laughed lightly. "I'm not sure how much help I'd be with that. But if that's what you need, then I'd be more than happy to stay and help out a bit until you can start using my marketing services."

Grady cringed as he realized he was backed into a corner. He'd assumed she would just outright refuse to do any manual labor, but she was now, in a roundabout way, saying she'd stay and help. Clara had just realized it too, and was staring at the other woman in horror.

"Of course, I will still spend my vacation with my friends here before they continue on without me. I've already had my things packed up and they're ready to be sent out here when I get settled again. I've missed you so much, and I can't wait to be back here where I belong."

Grady was sitting completely still, staring in disbelief. Janet had already planned on staying, and thought everything would go back to exactly how it had been when she left. He'd never felt more trapped in his life, but he couldn't say anything as long as everyone else was sitting around the table with them.

His grandma was standing in the open door-way, taking in the conversation. Her eyes moved slowly to Clara, who was now walking back toward the kitchen with empty plates in her hand. Her back was rigid, but she walked with a regal air that didn't show any of the pain he was sure she was feeling.

Everyone at the table started talking and asking him questions about the trail ride he was taking them on today. He tried to follow the conversation, and answer the best he could, but his heart had just walked out of the room without looking back.

He desperately wanted to go talk to Clara, and tell her none of this changed anything that was starting between them. Janet was in his past, even if she didn't know that. He wasn't going to let her charge back in here and destroy what he had with Clara.

And if it meant kicking all of his first paying customers out, he was willing to do it.

CHAPTER 15

"Thank you so much for all your help the past couple of days, Anne. Honestly, I don't know how I'd have managed without you. Grady was so busy with everything else, including the trail rides and interviews, it would have been difficult for me to do it all by myself."

They were washing the dishes by hand in the large tub they had on the counter. The guests had all finished their breakfast and were now upstairs packing to leave.

Well, most of them anyway.

Janet still insisted on staying, even though Clara knew Grady had mentioned more than once he really didn't need any help. But she was planning to stay here until she could get more suitable accommodations in town. After a couple of days with just the basics out here, she'd made it clear this wasn't the way she could live for much longer.

Clara hadn't had much time to be alone with Grady since the guests had arrived, although she did know he'd tried. She'd been so exhausted at the end of each day, she'd gone to bed early. And if she was being completely honest with herself, she may have been hiding a bit too.

She just wasn't sure she was ready to sit down and talk to him alone yet. She was afraid he'd tell her he had feelings for Janet still, while at the same time, she was afraid of him saying it was over with Janet and he wanted her. Then she'd have to make the decision about telling him the truth.

Either way, she wasn't sure how everything was going to work out. And she worried her heart was going to get damaged in the process.

"Oh, I'm certain you could have managed just fine. But thank you for letting me help and not complain about me getting in your way." Anne smirked at her as she picked up the coffee cup to dry.

"Have you had a chance to talk to Grady

alone since everyone got here? I know you're thinking the worst of him right now, but I can assure you, anything that was between him and Janet was over long ago. That girl was never right for him. I've never seen him as happy as he's been since you've been here. Just because Janet thinks he's going to welcome her back into his life with open arms, doesn't mean that's what he's going to do."

Clara swallowed and avoided Anne's gaze.

"I want to believe you, but sometimes I just look at her and can't understand how he could see past what she has that I don't. I hate feeling so insecure. I never used to be like this, but it seems since I've arrived here, I've just felt like I was so out of place."

"Do you love him?"

Clara dropped the cutlery she'd been washing back into the pan with a loud splash. She watched as the ripples moved across the water. "I don't know. I know my heart aches when I see him with Janet. I know every time he comes near me, I feel like my whole body lights up. And I know that when I'm with him, I feel so happy I could burst."

Anne gave a soft laugh. "Well then, my dear, I'd say you do know."

Lifting her eyes to Anne's, she smiled. "I guess I do."

The older woman set her towel down and placed her hand on Clara's arm, pulling gently to get her to turn and face her. "I don't know where you came from exactly, or the story of your past. But I know a heart that has found the one it was searching for. It doesn't matter what our pasts are, or what our differences are. What matters is how other people make us feel. In the end, that's truly all that does matter in this life. Just be yourself, and trust that Grady will be able to see your worth. Just because things might have been a bit different where you came from, what you feel in your heart is exactly the same. When you love someone, everything else can be overcome."

Clara stood facing Anne with her hands dripping on the floor. A lump moved into her throat, and she tried to find the words to thank the woman for everything she'd said. She was sure if she'd still had her mother, those were the exact words she'd have said to her.

"I'd give you a hug if I wasn't dripping water everywhere." She smiled at Anne, who stepped forward and put her arms around her.

"That's perfectly fine, my dear. I don't mind getting a little bit wet."

"Is everything okay in here?"

Grady's voice startled her, making her jump back out of Anne's embrace. She hadn't even heard him come into the house.

"Everything's fine. Just giving each other an encouraging hug to help us get through the rest of the dishes." Anne winked at Clara who had to laugh at the reason she gave him.

His eyebrow went up, and Clara's pulse pounded as she found herself being pulled into his dark gaze. "Well, hopefully you can manage now on your own for a bit. Now that the guests have left, I need a minute to talk to Clara alone."

He took her hand and pulled her with him, not even giving her or his grandmother a chance to argue.

"Where are we going? Can you please slow down so I don't feel like I'm being dragged along like a sack of flour?"

He stopped suddenly and turned. "When have you ever seen a sack of flour?"

Her heart jumped as he shook his head and smiled. "The things you say sometimes just make me scratch my head, but honestly, I think that's part of what makes me so crazy about you."

They were standing in the back of the house, with the leaves in the large trees around them swaying slightly while the creek trickled softly in the background.

She was wearing pants again today since the guests were leaving and there wasn't any excuse for her to stay in her dresses. She had hand-washed them both—the one she'd worn on the trip out west and the one she'd hoped to be married in. They were pegged on the line, drying in the fresh breeze blowing.

He reached out and tucked the loose hairs behind her ear that swirled around her face. Tipping his head slightly, he cupped her cheek with his palm.

"Clara, I want you to know that there is nothing between Janet and me anymore. She might like to believe there is, but I promise you, what we had ended long ago. Just because she's thrown herself back into my life, it doesn't mean I want her. I've recently discovered she's not my type at all."

The blood was rushing through her body as his thumb swirled on her jaw.

"And what exactly is your type?" She'd never been so forward talking to a man, but he was making her thoughts get all muddled up.

He brought his lips down to hers, and put his other arm around her waist to pull her in close to him. Her hands went onto his chest, and she timidly moved them up to go around his neck. As her fingers brushed the hair on the back of his head, he groaned.

When she was sure her legs wouldn't hold her any longer, he pulled his head back slightly and looked down into her eyes without blinking. Thankfully, he was still holding her so she didn't end up falling into a heap on the ground.

"Do you even have to ask that question?"

CHAPTER 16

"Thank you for letting me stay, Grady. I'm going to start looking for an apartment soon, but I'm also glad we will get some time to spend together too. I've really missed you."

Grady was out brushing down the horse he'd just rode back in on. He'd been out checking on some new calves that had been born, before hoping to find Clara to see if she'd like to take a walk.

He hadn't even heard Janet come into the stables.

Looking up, he was struck with how beautiful his high school sweetheart had become. She'd always been pretty, but she'd matured into a stunning woman. However, it was nothing like the beauty Clara had.

"It's no trouble. A paying customer is always welcome." He really didn't want her getting the wrong idea of why he'd allowed her to stay.

"Oh, Grady Langley, you wouldn't have thrown me out if I couldn't pay, and you know it. You always were too kindhearted. That's why you need someone like me helping you to make sure no one takes advantage of you. You're apt to charge too little, and even end up letting people stay for free if they give you some sad story about why they can't pay."

She'd always told him he was too soft, and a pushover. But his grandparents had raised him to be the kind of man who was honest and decent, and sometimes that meant needing to be a bit soft sometimes.

She tiptoed around the straw lying on the floor in front of the stall, moving over to the side he was standing on. She wore white sandals, and her perfectly manicured toes peeked out the ends.

"You really should wear better shoes in the barn. Can't promise you won't leave here with something on them you might not appreciate." He grinned to himself as he pictured her stepping in a large mound of manure with those sandals. There'd be nothing stopping it from getting onto her feet. He was sure she'd faint dead away.

"Very funny, Grady. I've been in these stables before, or don't you remember?"

He remembered, and he knew what she was talking about. This was the place where they'd shared their first kiss when they were seventeen-years-old.

Of course, back then she wasn't nearly as high-maintenance as he could see she was now. Although now that he thought about it, he realized she'd never really enjoyed being out here on the ranch. And he could remember her always complaining about the smell.

She scrunched her nose up as she reached out to use the stall panel to balance herself as she stepped over a large pile on the floor. "*Eww.* It still stinks as bad as I remember in here."

He shook his head and kept brushing the horse. What did she want anyway? This was the last place he thought she'd ever bother him.

"And I promise I'm still going to help around here. I know you mentioned more guests coming in a couple of days, so I will do my part to make sure everything is ready. Honestly, Clara seems to live in a different world. Just because the place is meant to portray a pioneer feel, it doesn't mean she couldn't pick up the pace a bit and do things a little more efficiently. Did you know I saw her washing her silly old dresses by hand? Why wouldn't she just put them into the machine on a delicate cycle? I mean, they're just costumes, so it's not like they're that expensive."

His body started to heat up with anger as Janet continued to talk. "I'd expect she appreciates the cost of everything, and doesn't want me to have to buy more. So I'm glad to hear she's taking such good care of things."

Janet rolled her eyes. "Well as long as I'm here, I'm going to make sure she's doing things properly."

He carefully set his brush down and stepped away from the horse, giving himself time to calm down before he started to speak.

"Janet, I appreciate your offer to help. And as long as you want to pitch in around here, you're more than welcome. However, when it comes to Clara, you will listen to her. She's the house manager, and she's the one who is in charge."

"Well, what kind of credentials does she even

have?" One hand went on her hip as she tilted her head to the side.

"I don't know about her credentials other than she does a great job here, and she's helped me immensely to get everything ready."

"You don't even know any of her background?"

"No, but I know enough to know I can trust her."

Janet was squinting her eyes now as she watched him. "Surely you're not involved with her romantically? She's not your type at all."

He sighed and turned to walk away. Her hands reached out and wrapped around his arm, stopping him.

"Janet, you're the one who left me, remember? So I'm not sure why you think you can come waltzing back in here like nothing happened. And while I was upset at the time, I have to honestly thank you now for doing what I didn't have the guts to do myself. You and I were never going to work out."

"How can you say that? I just needed some time to think and experience the world a bit. I always intended to come back."

He looked at her incredulously. She seriously didn't hear what he was trying to say.

"You and I are too different. You like being in the middle of all the action in town, and being the center of attention. That's never been who I was. I did it because I thought I was in love with you, and that was what I had to do. But I know now that while we may have been in love in high school, it wasn't the kind that could last. I need to be with someone who makes me feel alive, and lets me be who I am. Someone who is content to go for a horse ride and spend the day sitting under a tree."

Her eyes were slits as she listened to him. Before he knew what she was doing, she pushed herself forward and pressed up against him. Her arms went around his neck and she brought her lips to his.

He grabbed her arms and pulled them off, then stepped back. She stood staring at him with her lipstick smudged and her shoulders heaving. "Can your little girlfriend kiss you like that? Because from what I've seen of her, she likely hasn't even let you hold her hand yet."

"We are done, Janet. And I'm going to ask you to hurry and find yourself an apartment, because while I'm too much of a gentleman to throw you out like you deserve, I won't hesitate if you're still here by the weekend."

He stormed away, but he recognized the fury in her eyes. He just hoped she didn't decide to take it out on Clara.

If she did, she was about to finally see his harder side.

CHAPTER 17

*C*lara hummed softly to herself as she whipped the bed sheet out and threw it over the line. Now that she was more familiar with the washing machine, she'd managed to avoid any spills this time. But she still thought it was much nicer to have the bedding hung on the line to dry. She couldn't see how that hot air from the dryer could be any good for fabric.

"Clara, are you going to make lunch today or not? I'm starving." Janet's voice reached her ears, so she turned her head to see the woman standing on the back step. "Just because I've offered to help, doesn't mean I'm not still a paying guest who would like to be fed."

Clenching her teeth against the words she

wanted to say, Clara put the best smile on her face and walked back toward the house.

"I'm sorry, Janet. I wasn't sure what time you were getting up, so I hadn't set anything aside. I can warm up some soup and make a nice sandwich for you." She'd already eaten her lunch, but since she hadn't seen any sign of Janet, she'd assumed maybe she had left early and headed into town to look for an apartment.

Thankfully, the other woman must have been asleep by the time Grady had walked her back to the big house last night after they'd taken a ride together. It had been a wonderful ride, watching the setting sun and getting to be in each other's company without anyone around. And they hadn't brought Janet's name up once.

But when they'd got back, she could tell he'd been wary of leaving her in the house alone with her.

"I've been up for a while, but didn't figure there was any hurry to come down. Plus, some of us take some pride in our appearance and put some effort into how we'll look before our day starts."

Clara ignored the sting that Janet's words delivered.

She set the pot back on the stove, and poured some of the soup back in to warm it up.

"Is there honestly not a microwave around here you could use when there's no one else here to try giving the whole *pioneer experience* to?"

Clara had put up with abuse like this from Constance Dunning for years. She'd never treated her badly when her mom was around, but as soon as Lucy Dunning was out of earshot, Constance had made sure to remind Clara what her place was in the household.

So she'd learned how to put up a wall around herself to deflect the words that tried to hurt her. Obviously Janet wasn't happy about something, and she was determined to bring Clara into it.

Smiling, she turned and carried a mug to the table. "I've still got the coffee on the stove if you'd like some."

"No, I don't want any coffee." Janet was squinting at her and as Clara watched, something in her face seemed to soften. "I'm sorry for being such a grouch. I guess I'm just a bit overtired. It's been so strange coming back to Heartsbridge after all this time. But it's where I belong, and always have."

Nodding, Clara smiled at the other woman.

"I'm sure it's been tiring." The truth was, Clara couldn't really understand what was so tiring for her. It's not like she'd had to do anything since she'd arrived.

She turned to the stove and stirred the pot, then scooped some of the soup into a bowl. As she set it in front of Janet, the woman smiled warmly at her. "Why don't you sit down and join me for a bit? You could use a rest."

Clara really didn't want to sit and visit with her, but she couldn't be rude, so she pulled out a chair and sat down.

"It just feels so perfect to be back here with Grady, in the place where we grew up and fell in love. It feels like I never left. I can still see how he looks at me, and last night after he found me outside, we sat and talked until the wee hours of the morning. He told me how he had missed me, and how I'd been the only woman he'd ever been able to love."

Clara's stomach dropped to her feet. Janet had to be lying. Grady had never said he loved her, but she'd thought there was something starting to build between them. Surely he wouldn't have dropped her off after such a wonderful night together only to say those words to Janet?

"When last night? I wasn't aware you'd gone outside."

Janet waved her hand in front of her. "Well, I just couldn't sleep so I'd gone out to sit on the step. He was out for a late night walk I guess when he found me out there."

Clara tried to ignore the pounding in her ears as the blood rushed through her body.

"I asked him if he was seeing anyone else, and he said there was nothing serious with anyone. At least nothing that could ever compare to what we'd had. He said he'd just been waiting for me to come back into his life."

"But he told me it was over between you two." Clara hated how weak her voice sounded as she strangled the words out. Obviously Janet didn't realize Clara was in love with the man she was talking about.

"After we talked, he said he just couldn't ignore the old feelings. We've always had such chemistry together and we have a long history, with memories and feelings that can't be easily brushed aside. He's a good-looking man, and he deserves to have someone who shines beside him. That's always been me. We were meant to be together."

Clara was still having difficulty believing the woman. Grady had been so attentive to her when they'd been on their ride last night. And when he'd kissed her after they got back, she'd been sure it was filled with all of the feelings she was experiencing herself. Could a man be that quick to change his mind?

Her stomach churned as she tried to sort everything out in her head.

The sound of tires on the gravel outside drew her attention.

"Oh, I better hurry and get ready. Grady is taking me to town today so I can look for an apartment. He's taken the afternoon off so he can go with me. I just need to run up and get my sweater."

Clara couldn't move from the spot, feeling like her legs held heavy weights on them. Grady came through the door, offering her a smile, but she couldn't stand and greet him.

He looked nervous as he looked at her. "I told Janet I'd take her to town today to see if she can find an apartment since she doesn't have her own car here. But we shouldn't be too long."

Janet rushed into the room. "I'm all ready to go."

Grady was still staring at her, not even acknowledging the other woman and she could see him swallow as his forehead creased together with concern.

"Clara?"

She gave her head a slight shake to try and clear the dizziness. Offering the best smile she could put on, she stood up and started to clean the dishes from the table. "Have fun. I'll see you when you get back." Her words sounded flat even to her own ears.

This wasn't fair. She had to trust him, and believe in the kind of man she'd seen him to be since she'd met him. Grady wouldn't do this to her.

"Clara, would you mind washing the bedding in my room? I love the fresh smell of them hanging outside to dry. It might help me sleep better tonight." Janet walked toward the front door. When she realized Grady was still standing watching Clara, she stopped and turned around. "Are you coming, Grady?"

"Clara, are you all right?" His eyes searched hers.

She needed to believe him. Giving him a

genuine smile, she nodded. "Yes, I'm fine. I will see you later."

Finally, he nodded and followed Janet out the door. Clara leaned back against the counter and tried to calm her breathing. She wasn't going to let Janet make her believe that Grady had said any of those things.

But why would she lie to her?

She decided she better get the bedding from Janet's room so it had time to dry. Climbing the stairs, she made her way to the room at the end of the hall, opposite to the side her room was on. When she went inside, she cringed at the mess. There was makeup all over the counter by the mirror, and clothes draped over every inch of the room.

She went to the bed and pulled back on the sheet, noticing an opened piece of paper sitting by the pillow. She didn't mean to look, but she immediately recognized Grady's scribbled handwriting and his name signed at the bottom.

Her heart sunk as her knees gave out beneath her and she sat on the edge of the bed. With trembling hands, she picked up the note addressed to Janet. She knew she shouldn't be reading it, but her eyes seemed to have a mind of their own.

As the tears started to fall, she fought to continue reading the words on the paper.

Now she knew that everything Janet had told her was true. Grady was still in love with her, and he planned to make a life with her.

Anything Clara had believed to be between them had been nothing more than her own foolish notions.

CHAPTER 18

*I*t had been a long afternoon, but thankfully he'd managed to help Janet find an apartment she could move into soon. If her family hadn't moved away right after high school, he would have just sent her there to stay. But it wasn't available until the weekend, so she'd have to spend a couple of more nights at the B and B.

He had more guests registered to arrive tomorrow, so he just hoped Janet could stay out of the way enough and not cause any problems for Clara.

His stomach had been in knots all day, because he'd known something was up when he saw her earlier, but he didn't have the time to stay and find out. He intended to find her as soon as they were back and make sure everything was all right.

As they pulled up in front of the big house, he noticed there was only a small lamp on the front porch. The rest of the house was in darkness as the sun made its way down below the horizon. He knew they'd taken longer than he'd hoped, but he was surprised Clara would have gone to bed so early.

When they got out, Janet stormed toward the house. She'd spent the entire day trying to work her charms on him, but he'd done nothing but ignore her, speaking to her only when necessary. A part of him was sad that the girl he'd thought he'd loved for so many years had turned into a woman like this.

And he thanked his lucky stars he'd dodged that bullet.

He walked up the front steps and jumped when the door was flung open before he could reach the knob. His grandma stood in the doorway wringing her hands with worry. His grandpa was right behind her and they stepped out onto the porch.

Janet tried to move past them, but his grandpa put his hand out to stop her. "I think you might want to stay here a moment, young lady. There's something we all need to talk about."

Grady looked at the seriousness of his grandpa's face.

"What's going on? I'm tired, and I need to have a minute with Clara, then I'm headed to bed myself." But something in the way his grandparents looked at him stopped him cold.

"Well, earlier this afternoon, after you had left, Clara came up to the house. She said she needed to take her dress in to have Moira do some work on it. I offered to do it for her, but she said it was something only Moira could fix. I figured maybe she was lonesome for a friend, and since I needed a few things anyway, I said I could take her."

"Why didn't she just ask to come in with me to visit Moira while I was in town?" He was kicking himself for not thinking that she might need to see her friend once in a while, and she'd been stuck out here on her own so much.

His grandmother looked like she'd lost her best friend. "She said she'd just get Moira to give her a ride home. So I left her there."

"Grandma, what are you getting at? I really don't see the big deal about her going in to visit Moira."

"She's not back yet, Grady. And when I dropped her off, something didn't seem right. When she said goodbye to me, it felt like it was going to be more than just a few hours she was leaving. She seemed so sad."

Now his heart was starting to pump faster as he realized what his grandma might be saying. The pit in his stomach started to grow.

"Well, this is none of my concern, so if you don't mind, I'm heading to bed. I told you she wasn't right for you, Grady, and I guess this just proves it." Janet went to take a step, but his grand-father was still holding his hand on her arm.

He pulled a sheet of paper out from behind his back with his other arm, and handed it to Grady. "No, I think you'd better stay."

He turned to face his grandson. "After Anne got back, she was so worried. We waited for Moira's car to come up the drive, but never saw it. I decided to come down to the big house to check on things and get the fire going in case Clara showed up later. I didn't want her to have to do it on her own. I found this sitting on the table in the kitchen."

Grady was already reading the words on the paper and his world was starting to spin around him as he realized what had happened. He lifted his eyes to Janet's. "Why is this sitting out on the table? Why do you even still have it?"

Janet was crying now, hoping for some sympathy that he didn't have in him to give right now. He was angry, and no tears were going to change that.

"Well, she must have found it in my room. She had no business snooping. It's not like I did it on purpose."

Everything was starting to make sense. "You asked her to change your bedding. You left it where you knew she would find it."

"Grady, her heart was likely broken reading that letter. How could you have done that to her?" His grandfather's voice was angry.

"I didn't. This letter was one I wrote to Janet years ago, after we'd had a fight. I'd been flirting with a girl one night when we went out to a party, and she was mad. She'd gone to spend some time with her cousin in Austin, but when she got back, we made up. I wrote it to her when I was still young and foolish and thought she was the kind of person I could spend the rest of my life with. Apparently she held on to that letter and decided to use it to try getting her way one more time."

He had to sit down as the pounding in his head became louder. What must Clara have thought after reading that letter? He looked back down at the paper that was held in his trembling hands.

Dear Janet,

I'm so glad you're back. You have no idea how much I missed you. Every time I see you, my heart feels like the missing piece has been returned.

You're the only woman I could ever love the way I do. I know I messed up, and I promise to spend the rest of my life making it up to you. There's no one else, and there never could be anyone who could take your place. That other girl could never compare to you.

The only eyes I want to be looking into are yours. No one else will ever have my heart.

Now that you're home again, let's start building our future together.

Love always and forever,

Grady

He was sure he was going to be sick. He'd written this note as a lovesick nineteen-year-old boy who didn't know any better. Lifting his eyes to Janet, he ground out between clenched teeth, "I want you to get your things. I'm headed into

Moira's to find Clara and I'll be dropping you off at a hotel. You have ten minutes to pack."

As Janet flew into the house, sobbing loudly, his grandma came over and put her hand on his shoulder. "There's more, Grady, and I think you better stay sitting for the rest."

CHAPTER 19

His heart in his throat, he warily watched as his grandmother came to sit beside him. She was holding an album of some kind in her hands that he hadn't even noticed until now.

"There was something about Clara that had always bothered me, and I couldn't quite put my finger on it."

"I thought you adored Clara. You both seemed to hit it off so well." He was shocked to hear his grandma say she was bothered by her.

"Oh, I did. Clara is a wonderful girl. I meant there was something that just wasn't adding up. When I first heard her name, it struck me as odd, because I was sure I'd heard her name before.

One night, I realized it was from one of the stories from years gone by. I knew there was a newspaper article that had made it down through the generations in the safe, so I went to look at it to see if I was remembering correctly." She opened the album and pointed to the old newspaper clipping that was pressed safely between a plastic sleeve.

He remembered seeing this years ago when the family had gotten together, and talk had ended up going back to the old legends. It was an article about how Noah Langley and his sister Charlotte had been involved in bringing one of the biggest crooks in Heartsbridge history to justice.

His grandma placed her finger on the spot she wanted him to read. "Right there."

Martin Paine was awaiting his new bride to arrive from Boston, a woman named Clara Swanson. When Gabe Noland found out, he decided to take matters into his own hands, and kidnapped a woman he believed to be this Paine's intended bride.

The story went on as Grady remembered it, but his eyes were stuck on the name of the intended bride.

Clara Swanson.

"Well, I guess it could be some family of hers. She mentioned she came from Boston."

He wasn't sure why his breathing was becoming more labored. This was all so confusing.

"That's what I thought, but then little things started to stand out to me. The day she tried to open the can of Coke and truly acted as though she'd never seen it before. Little things she would say, like how she'd been a maid for a family in Boston. I couldn't believe it could be true, but something just seemed so off, and I had to find out."

His grandma squeezed his hand. "After I dropped her off at Moira's today, I went to the public library to go through some of their archive machines. I pulled up some papers from Boston around the same time as the story about this Clara Swanson. It took me some time, but I found a society paper that published a story about a scandal that broke out not long after Clara would have arrived to meet her husband. Apparently a wealthy businessman was found to be "fraterniz-ing" with the maid, and his wife had thrown him out on his ear. When I read the article, it mentioned there was a rumor he'd been trying to force himself on another maid who'd previously been in their employ, a woman named Clara Swanson."

He was having trouble focusing as she reached into her pocket and pulled out her cell phone. "I took a picture of the image they'd posted of the former maid. It was taken a few months prior, while at some event to celebrate his business."

Looking down at the phone, somehow he already knew what he was going to see. The picture was fuzzy, a combination of the primitive cameras of the time and the attempt by his grandmother to get a picture for her phone.

But staring back at him through the screen were the eyes he'd looked into so many times before.

His thoughts were in a whirlwind in his mind. "The washing machine. Her saying she had no electricity growing up. The dress she wore." He looked helplessly at his grandparents. *Surely this wasn't true.*

His grandpa put his hand on his shoulder. "I've told you the stories about my own grandfather. I never knew for sure, but now I do. Somehow, my grandpa, my great-aunt, and now Clara too, were able to move through time. I can't understand it any more than you, but I'd suggest you stop and think hard about how you're going to find her before it's too late."

Grady stared back down at the phone he held in his hands. Suddenly, a memory burst through his mind as clear as the day it happened.

He could see the light flash under the door at the diner, and the woman lying on the couch in the back. He saw the rustle of blue silk fabric. At the time, he was sure he could see the hair of the woman as she moved, but this time, as though he was standing right beside the couch, he could see her eyes.

It was Clara. And that's how she'd gotten here.

His stomach sunk as he realized, that's also how she'd likely try to go back.

~

HE DIDN'T EVEN WAIT for Janet. Hopping into his truck, he drove straight to Moira's, praying he wasn't too late. He'd tried calling numerous times, but each time Moira's voice told him to leave a message.

All the lights were off in the diner.

134

Please, just let her be staying with Moira in her apartment. He kept repeating the words over and over in his mind, hoping it would make it true. He went to the back, taking the outside stairs up to her apartment two at a time. When he got to the top, the faint glow of a lamp shone in a window.

He knocked loudly. "Moira, it's Grady Langley."

It seemed to take forever before the door opened. When it did, it looked like Moira had been crying and he was sure new tears were starting to make their way down her cheeks.

She shook her head slowly. "It's too late, Grady. She's gone."

No, he didn't believe her.

He moved past Moira into the apartment. "Clara, are you here?"

He was met with nothing but silence. He turned back to Moira, waiting for her to tell him something, anything, he could do to find her.

"I know the truth, Moira, and now I need to know what I can do to get her back."

Moira closed her eyes briefly, as though she was in pain. "I tried to tell her to wait, to give you a chance to talk to her and explain everything. But she said she didn't belong here and would never be what you needed anyway. She was just tired of having to lie and she said she couldn't stand to stay here and know you didn't love her." She moved over and sat down on her couch. "This is the first time the two hearts we brought together didn't stay together. You found each other, and I thought it would work out. I feel like I've failed."

"I'm not entirely sure what you're talking about, Moira. But I'm not letting her go. So you better figure out how I can get to her."

She looked down at a timepiece she had pulled out from the collar of her blouse. "The hands are still moving, but they're slowing down."

"What are you talking about? What does that do?."

"It's how we move people between time periods. We could try sending you there, Grady, but I don't know if it will work. And if it does, who knows what will happen after that. Usually once the hands slow down, it means the opening through time is about to close for that person. And when the hands stop moving, there's no going back. I've never had to send the one person after another, so I don't know if it will work."

"We have to try. I can't just let her go." His heart was already aching with the pain of what he knew Clara believed. He couldn't let her think he didn't love her.

Moira stood up, still holding the timepiece. "If you go, you won't have much time. Once the hands stop, you could be stuck there. Are you sure?"

He nodded his head. "I've never been more sure of anything in my life."

CHAPTER 20

Clara sat under the small tree next to the creek, listening to the sound of the infant beside her as he babbled and laughed. She had to smile at the innocence of the baby as he tried to take his first few steps on his own.

"Oh, Henry, you are a sweetheart."

The woman on the blanket beside her laughed softly. "Yes, he is. Most of the time." She put her hand on her growing belly and looked down. "And I'm sure this one will be too."

It still seemed so strange to be sitting here beside Grady's great-great-grandmother, and to be at the same farm she'd just left, except a century earlier. She could see the same trees, some of them just saplings that would become large, towering trees surrounding the house that would stand nestled among them. At the moment, the small cabin Grady had told her about was all that was here.

There was so much life to be lived between now and then.

Noah walked over from putting the last of the feed out for the animals, and bent down to kiss Elizabeth on the top of her head, before sitting down beside her. When he smiled at his wife, Clara's heart ached, knowing the love they shared was something she would never know.

Her heart match had been Grady, she had no doubt about that. But something had gone wrong for their happy ending, and now she'd never be able to get back to him.

"I can't thank you both enough for letting me spend the day here. I know it all must seem strange, but I just felt like I needed to be close to him one more time before I continue on my way. I'm not going back to Boston, but I can't stay here either with the memories and the surroundings haunting me."

"Well, it was nice of you to share some of the stories that let us know how much of an impact we will have on future generations. Although, I have to say, I'm not particularly impressed with that great-great-grandson of mine. I just can't figure out how he could be the kind of man who could hurt a woman he cared for." Noah shook his head as he reached out to help Henry who was now crawling onto his lap.

Elizabeth frowned at her husband. "Noah, we don't know the whole truth. We weren't there, and we don't know what happened." She quickly turned to pat Clara on the leg. "Not that I don't trust you, Clara, but I just feel there's something that doesn't sound right to me. I believe that if your hearts were destined to be together, and it truly sounds to me like they were, then it just doesn't make sense that his heart would stray."

Clara looked out to the pen where a few animals were milling around. It was a beautiful day, and it reminded her of the day she'd stood in almost this very spot in Grady's arms. She'd asked him what his type was, and he'd held her close and left her breathless as his lips had found hers. In that moment, she'd never been happier. She'd been so sure everything was going to work out, and her heart had found the one it was supposed to be with.

The ache in her chest deepened as she fought against the memories that contradicted everything she'd read in that note. The words Janet had said to her had left her with wounds as she battled the doubt, not wanting to believe the worst.

But that note had taken away any of the doubt she'd had.

"You know, when I first ended up in this time, I struggled to figure out so much about how to live without the means I'd become accustomed to. And for my sister Charlotte, it was even harder. She was used to wearing pants, and clothing that was so different to this time. She still wears pants around the farm when it's just her and Gabe, but when she goes out in public, she's willing to dress the way it's expected of her. She says it's getting easier." Noah was smiling at her as he struggled to keep Henry from stealing his hat. Finally giving in, he let the child pull it from his head, revealing dark hair that reminded Clara so much of the man she'd left behind.

The eyes that were smiling into hers bore the resemblance too, and her heart squeezed with pain as it tried not to remember.

"Yes, it was hard to fit in. I never felt like I could belong." It was nice to have someone who could understand.

"I hope you know it would have gotten easier,

over time. And if you'd told Grady the truth, he might have been able to help you adjust." His eyes weren't moving from hers, and she almost felt like Grady was sitting there himself.

Swallowing hard, she shrugged. "I never got the chance to tell him. I would have, but I was too afraid of what he'd say. What if he didn't believe me?"

Elizabeth chuckled. "Oh, I know from experience how hard it is to believe something like this, but I also know that when your heart belongs to someone, you give yourself completely. And that includes trusting that they will tell the truth."

They sat for a moment listening to the water making its way along the path it had carved into the ground, while the birds in the trees above them sang cheerfully to each other.

"Were you so afraid of never fitting in, that you just took the first reason you could find to leave? Did you ever give Grady the chance to try and explain?" Noah's voice reached her ears, and she closed her eyes briefly as she tried not to let the truth in his words affect her.

"Sometimes, things aren't what they seem. It sounds to me like you left without finding out the truth from Grady. If your hearts were matched through time, there's nothing that should have come between you. But I think maybe you let a woman who doesn't care a wit about you, play into your own insecurities, enough to push you away from the one person who I'm sure would have moved heaven and earth to be with you."

Her chin started to tremble as she realized how right Noah was. She'd let Janet make her believe something that didn't make sense, all because she was so afraid she'd never fit in with the world Grady lived in.

She'd never given him the chance to explain. After everything, she'd left without even saying goodbye.

Her heart shattered as the pain of it all finally took over. Tears made their way down her cheeks as she suffered through the loss of what could never be.

"And now it's too late." The words barely made it above a whisper.

She turned to look at the couple who were watching her closely. Noah lifted his shoulder and shook his head.

"I don't ever believe in it being too late. If there's a way to get back to him, you need to find out. Cissie is the only one who can help you."

A spark of hope ignited in her. "Do you think there's a way?"

"I have no idea. But I know if it were me, there's nothing I wouldn't do to try."

Clara was already on her feet, crossing the yard to where she'd tied the horse she'd ridden out on this morning from Cissie's.

Noah and Elizabeth followed close behind. Flinging her leg over the saddle in a very unlady-like manner, she smiled warmly down at the couple. "Thank you."

She bent down to hug Elizabeth, and turned her eyes to Noah.

"If you can't get back, you're always welcome here. But if you get back to him, always remember your worth and give him the chance to show you his love."

She nodded, then kicked her horse toward the road that would lead her back to Heartsbridge. She didn't know if there was any way to get back to Grady, but she was going to do everything she could to try.

CHAPTER 21

The hooves pounded the ground beneath her as she raced out of the yard. Cissie had said the hands were still moving this morning, however they were getting slower, so Clara didn't know if they would have stopped yet or not.

Why had she been so quick to make her decision to leave? She should have trusted her own heart; and not let that woman get into her head.

Finally making it to the road, she turned toward town, urging her horse to move faster. As she looked ahead, she could make out a figure on a horse riding in her direction. Maybe it was Cissie, and she'd be able to get her back.

When they got closer though, she could see it was a man and the dust that was being kicked into the air showed he was riding like the devil was on his heels.

Suddenly, her heart leaped into her throat as she recognized the man in the saddle.

"Grady!" His name tore from her lips as she pulled on the reins, jumping from the back of the horse before it had even completely stopped. She ran the rest of the way as his horse pranced sideways at the sudden stop.

Within seconds, she was in his arms, crying his name over and over. When she pulled back, he smiled down into her face and reached up to wipe the tears that were rolling down her cheeks.

"For someone who went an awful long way to get away, you sure seem happy to see me."

"I'm so sorry. I wasn't thinking. I just heard Janet say you had told her she was the one you loved, and all the worries I had about whether I'd ever be good enough for you took over. Then, when I saw that note, I couldn't think straight."

They stood on the side of the road, with the dust from their horses hooves settling around them. He was holding her close and her arms were on his shoulders as she lifted her eyes to his.

"Clara, you should have known I wasn't the

kind of man who would ever do that to you. You've had my heart since the day I saw you lying on a couch in a flash of blue silk. And every day I've spent with you has shown me what love is. I would never have done anything to throw that away."

She didn't want to bring it up, but she had to know. "But, the letter?"

He rolled his eyes and the muscles in his jaw tightened as he shook his head. "That was a note written by a boy to the girl he thought he loved many years ago. But I never loved Janet in the way I love you, Clara. You are the other half of my heart."

His lips gently touched hers, but she could feel the strength of the emotion behind them.

"How did you get here?"

"The hands were still moving, so Moira let me try. I couldn't just let you go without telling you the truth."

She'd been so foolish, and now Grady might be stuck here. "But, what if we can't get back? Your grandparents, the B and B you've worked so hard to build…" The shame of what she'd done made her whole body feel numb.

But Grady just laughed quietly and reached

up to push her hair back from her forehead. "It doesn't matter. As long as I have you."

The sound of hooves pounding the ground broke the spell she was under and she pulled away to see who was coming toward them. "Cissie?"

"Thanks for waiting, Grady. I was sure I was going to find you with a broken neck somewhere along the way." Cissie's shoulders heaved as though she'd been the one running. "We have to hurry. They've almost stopped."

Grady stepped back and turned his head to look in the direction of the farm she'd just left. She could see the struggle he faced as he realized he could have the chance to meet the ancestor of his who'd left such an impact on his own life. He could see the farm from where they stood on the road, and as she watched, his eyes scanned every square inch of land.

He was seeing the place where he'd grown up, the ranch he called home, when it was just getting started.

But there wasn't time to go any closer.

As they stood on the road, her eyes were drawn to movement next to the tree where moments earlier she'd been sitting with Noah and Elizabeth. Grady's eyes followed, and as they watched from the distance, the couple raised their hands to give a small wave.

Somehow, they knew who this was, and it warmed Clara's heart to know they were all getting a small glimpse into the past and the future.

"Grady. Clara. You need to decide. I don't know if we're going to make it." Cissie still sat on her horse watching them.

Grady brought his hand down from waving back at the couple next to the tree, then quickly turned and grabbed Clara around the waist, throwing her into the saddle, before jumping up behind her. "I'm not taking any chances of you getting away on me before we get back."

Kicking his heels in, they raced toward town.

This time, Cissie was keeping up, and Clara prayed they weren't too late.

When they arrived at the boardinghouse, they all jump down and ran inside. As they got into the back room, Cissie looked down at the timepiece. "I hope it's not too late. It's barely moving."

When she went to leave the room, Grady stopped her. "What about Clara's dress? The blue one?"

Cissie creased her eyes together in confusion. "It's in her room. You don't have time to get it."

"We need that dress. I want her to wear it when we get married."

Cissie seemed to understand how important it was, and ran from the room.

"Grady, this is silly. I don't need that dress to get married."

"No, you don't. But somehow I think it's important to you."

She swallowed as the feelings threatened to choke her.

Cissie flew back into the room, thrusting the dress into her hands. Before she ran back out, she stopped and turned to look at them. "I wish you both happiness and love." She smiled and disappeared.

A flash of light took over much the same way as it had the other times, although nowhere near as bright. This time though, when she opened her eyes again, she was looking into the face of the man she loved.

"Did we make it back?"

He smiled down at her. "I don't know. But whatever happened, as long as you're in my arms, I'll be a happy man."

EPILOGUE

The warm breeze gently tickled her skin as she turned her face up to the man beside her. The leaves in the trees rustled together as they moved, while she listened to the voice of the man saying the vows that would bind them together for life.

"You may kiss the bride."

A wide grin spread across his face as he pulled her into his arms. When his head dipped down, the shade from his cowboy hat hid the heat she knew was evident on her cheeks. As his lips touched hers, she pulled him closer, moving her own in time with his.

Suddenly, the voices of the people in attendance who were cheering at the newly married couple broke through the moment.

He lifted his head slightly and smiled down at her. "Tell me again why we didn't just elope somewhere by ourselves?"

She pretended to slap his arm as she pulled back to face the friends and family who were standing and clapping.

The yard had been decorated with silk flowers and ribbon, thanks mostly to Anne and Moira who'd taken it upon themselves to be the wedding planners. The tree they stood under was the same tree she'd sat with Noah and Elizabeth just a few short days ago.

Somehow, as they had stood saying their vows in the yard where Grady's ancestors had spent their lives together, Clara had sensed them both there.

The guests all got up to start the celebrating, and Anne came over to put her arms around Clara. "Welcome to the family, my dear. I feel like you've been sent here for all of us."

She smiled warmly at the older woman as she hugged her back. "Thank you, Anne. You have no idea how good it feels to have a family now."

Grady's grandfather reached out to pull her away from Anne, and brought her in for a hug too. "Well, we are your family now, and I'm so happy to have you."

Coming from a man who was normally reserved and quiet, Clara's heart warmed at his words.

Some of the other family members came over to be introduced, and Clara was eventually pulled away from Grady. Now and then, she would look over and catch him smiling at her, and her cheeks would burn with the promise she could see in his eyes.

By the end of the evening, she had to sit under the tree and rest for a moment. She folded her legs beneath her and sat on the ground, resting her back against the trunk. Her eyes moved around the celebration in front of her, and her heart almost burst with fullness.

The glowing lights that were strung between the trees and poles placed around the area lit up the night with an orange hue. People were dancing and laughing, and behind it all, the B and B stood reflected against the night sky.

"Can I join you?"

Grady's voice made her jump. She'd been so lost in her thoughts she hadn't even heard him walk over to her.

"Of course." She smiled and lifted her hand out to him.

He sat beside her, bringing his knees up and resting his arms on them as he leaned slightly forward.

"You looked beautiful today." He turned his head slightly and smiled at her.

They'd only been back for a few days, and Grady had insisted he was marrying her immediately. She'd worn her blue dress, the one she'd always planned to wear when she was married. And so she wouldn't feel out of place, he'd insisted everyone else was to wear the clothing to suit the time of the B and B.

He'd told her as long as she was comfortable wearing the clothes she was used to, he didn't care. He just wanted her to be happy and to feel like she belonged.

She'd wear the clothes she was used to at the B and B, their new home, but anywhere else, she would try to get used to the clothes from this time.

"Janet didn't waste much time going back to New York after she realized you were marrying me."

He cringed as he rolled his eyes. "Can we not bring her up today? I still can't believe how close she came to destroying my chance at happiness."

He reached out and pulled her over, moving in behind her so she was leaning back against his chest. His arms held her tight, and she could feel his heart beating against her back.

"I guess now I understand what the note was about that Noah left in the wall. He must have known I was going to do this to the house after talking with you, and hoped maybe I could spare the heartache we both went through when you left. It was his way of letting me know that love would win."

"I still can't believe how much you risked by coming back to get me. You had so much to lose."

His fingers started to move, caressing the silky fabric covering her arms. As she spoke, he stopped and his hands came up to her shoulders, forcing her to turn back to look at him.

"Clara, how can you say that? Can't you understand by now that when you left, I had already lost everything? I couldn't have lived knowing I hadn't tried to get you."

His hand reached up and his thumb moved across her lips. She had to remind herself to keep breathing as she found herself lost in his gaze.

As their lips met, she was sure she could hear the faint sound of a clock ticking out the time. Everything seemed to spin for a moment, and she had to pull back to see what had happened.

Grady looked down at her with the love reflected in his eyes. How could she ever have doubted how he felt?

In the whisper of the breeze, she was sure she could hear a familiar voice speaking.

"And would move heaven and earth to be with you."

She realized how right Noah had been. Grady had done exactly that, and as she looked up into the dark eyes smiling down at her, she knew without a doubt, this was where her heart belonged.

∽

I HOPE you enjoyed Timeless Devotion…if you could head back to Amazon and leave a review, it would be greatly appreciated!

If you'd like to read Noah and Elizabeth's story that started it all, go to my website KayPDawson.com and click to get "Timeless Spirit".

ALSO BY KAY P. DAWSON

Go to my Book Listing page under "My Books" on my website for all of my books, and latest releases!

KayPDawson.com

**My 13 year old daughter has tried her hand at writing western romance...if you'd like to take a look at the book that has received amazing reviews - professionally edited and formatted (but left entirely in her 13 year old voice and views).

You can find her books listed under Morgan Dawson on my website.

Made in the USA
Coppell, TX
27 April 2025

48704270R10100